The Golem of Rhodes

A further tale of the *sica*

Jonathan Harries

RHINO BOOKS

Rhino Books
An imprint of Jonathan Harries Ink
250 West Street Apt 5E
New York, NY 10013

www.jonathanharriesink.com

ISBN (e-book): 978-1-950628-22-3
ISBN (print): 978-1-950628-21-6

First edition

Contents

To Noni, and all the victims of hatred and bigotry in Rhodes.

Preface

As I looked back at my life during one particularly nasty bout of insomnia, I realized how many of its twists and turns have been determined by the decision-making strategy known as *satisficing*. If you're unfamiliar with this term, just split it somewhere down the middle and you'll see it's a combination of the words *satisfying* and *sufficing*.

You could sum up the meaning of *satisficing* this way: "Don't waste your time looking for the sharpest needle in the haystack, just one sharp enough to sew the rip in your trousers." Not that I'd pick up a needle myself—why would I when the old lady at the corner dry cleaners does a fine job? She isn't as good as the tailor my wife goes to, but for me, she is perfectly adequate. I've found *satisficing* to be an excellent concept when deciding how much effort to put into any aspect of my daily regimen. It's efficient and rarely disappoints.

You might be wondering just how I apply this principle to my books on my family's nearly two-thousand-year-old assassination business, and I'm happy to enlighten you. It's all to do with the amount of energy I've had to put into researching the accuracy of the stories: enough to believe they're authentic, but not enough to prove it.

In the first book in the series, *The Tailor of Riga,* the information I needed to weave the disturbing story of events that ranged from the killing of Jack the Ripper to a failed attempt on the life of Lenin came from my parents, who filled me in on the family history on the eve of my seventeenth birthday just before I went off to become a mercenary and bodyguard to Jean-Bodel Bokassa, the cannibal president of the Central African Republic. My mother's diary and my father's memoirs of his time in India provided sufficient context and nuance to make their stories credible.

The subsequent books—*The Carpet Salesman from Baghdad, The Bodyguard of Sarawak, The Correspondent of Petrograd,* and *The Mercenary of Urga*—all stemmed from diaries and notes either sent to me by relatives in different countries or records discovered by happenstance hidden in an old three-volume set of *The Adventures of Haji Baba of Ispahan.* Wikipedia and other online resources were all I needed to confirm certain details and make the stories plausible.

When I'd completed The Mercenary of Urga, I came to the inevitable conclusion that nothing more about the family was going to be as easily available as it had been and that the only way I'd uncover more stories about my ancestral assassins would be to visit relatives around the world to see if, per chance, they had records or documents buried in their attics. Clearly, this course would have required more effort than I wished to expend, and so I settled down to watching Netflix, listening to history podcasts, and reading, all the while hoping for something to fall into my laptop. I'm pleased to report that it didn't take long for serendipity to poke me in the eye.

It did so one morning in the form of a book from my daily BookBub reading suggestions email. The book in question was a lengthy one on the Greek Civil War that took place from 1946 to 1949. It was not an event I knew much about, and because it was only $1.99 for the Kindle version, I bought it.

In the middle of Chapter 6 (which is as far as I got), I came across a reference to the Greek Jews, a majority of whom were killed in the Holocaust, and more specifically, a group called the Romaniotes. This Jewish community, one of the oldest in all of Europe, can trace its lineage to around 300-25 BCE, and its name, "Romaniote," refers to the Eastern Roman Empire of which it was a part. Members settled in Thessaloniki, Athens, Corinth, Ioannina, and on the islands of Corfu, Crete, Samos, and Rhodes, where they became an integral and respected part of their communities.

I was given a firsthand account of the Jews of Rhodes, specifically those who'd been driven out of Spain by the Inquisition in 1492, by my step-daughter-in-law's grandmother, the much-loved "Noni," whose family was one of the very few Jewish families of Rhodes who managed to escape the Holocaust. I spent a delightful, if intense, couple of hours listening to her stories, and she left me with an unscratchable itch to learn more—most importantly about how a community that numbered nearly six thousand before the Italian Fascists drove many of them away and the Nazis sent the remainder to Auschwitz existed harmoniously with the Greeks and Ottomans on Rhodes for hundreds of years. The truth, as I discovered, was that they hadn't, and the event that perhaps epitomized their tragedy was the 1840 Blood Libel of Rhodes.

I grew up in a secular family where religion was rarely discussed, let alone practiced. I am not by any means religious, though I am intensely fascinated by religion. More specifically, by why some people have faith in the unknowable but are skeptical of the known and why certain religions preach love but eructate hatred for those who worship differently to them.

Antisemitic tropes, of which blood libels are part, have been used to defame and dehumanize Jews for centuries. The first recorded blood libel occurred in England in 1144, when the death of a young boy was blamed on the Jews of Norwich. The community was accused of ritually killing the boy so that his blood could be used to make matzos for the Passover feast. Many of the Norwich Jews were massacred, and the event ultimately led to the expulsion of the Jews from England in 1290.

Blood libels continued well into the twentieth century—all bizarre and senseless—but the one that took place in Rhodes sent me scurrying down an endless rabbit hole of research. It was not the barbarity of the treatment of the Jews accused and tortured by members of the Greek Orthodox church, Ottoman officials, and some European consuls that jolted me out of my sedentary state but rather the identity of the man dispatched to exact revenge on the accusers.

The deeper I dived into this mysterious figure sent to Rhodes by Abdülmecid I, the seventeen-year-old Sultan of the Ottoman Empire, to avenge the atrocities, the more I wanted to believe that he might have been David Smulian-Hasson, the father of Elias Smulian-Hasson, the central figure in my book, *The Carpet Salesman from Baghdad*, a distant relative of my mother. The stealth of the assassin, the methodology he employed, and the nature of the wounds of the victims—perfectly severed kidneys—were all too reminiscent of the technique used by the Smulian side of our family. Of course, all of this was happy speculation on my part. Nothing in what I read confirmed the identity of the assassin.

Then one night when I was once again having difficulty sleeping, I started to reread some of the emails I'd received after the publication of *The Carpet Salesman from Baghdad*. Most were from irate members of my family who were pissed as hell at me for portraying the family as a bunch of bloodthirsty assassins. There was one, however, from a lawyer in Paris, which I'd ignored at the time. Now, I'm not sure why I ignored it—most likely because I was numb from all the threats and ill-will—but it contained an inkling that became the core of this story.

The lawyer, Anna Crémieux, is a descendant of Isaac Crémieux, one of the two Jewish notables (the other being Sir Isaac Montefiore of England) who had journeyed together to Constantinople in 1840 to implore the sultan to intervene in the cases against the Jews of Rhodes and Damascus, where another blood libel had occurred at around the same time. Fortunately for me, the lawyer had not taken umbrage at my lack of response and was only too happy to provide me with the confirmation (a simple paragraph in the diary of her long-deceased relative) that I needed to feel confident that the protagonist in this story was indeed David Smulian-Hasson.

Here's the excerpt in question:

> *Both Montefiore and I were advised by an agent of David Sassoon, the great Jewish merchant of Bombay, to recommend to Reşid Pasha, vizier of the sultan, a man by the name of David Smulian-Hasson, whom he most fervently believed would be able to avenge the injustices visited upon the Jews of Rhodes. Montefiore referred to this man as a golem.*[1]

What follows is the story of an assassin armed with a peculiar sickle-shaped dagger known as the *sica* that had been my family's tool of trade since their expulsion from the Tribe of Asher in Judea around 80 AD. Together with Crémieux's simple paragraph (translated by my friend Mathieu Lignel), I was able to piece the account together

---

[1] *From the diary of Isaac-Jacob Adolphe Crémieux, Paris, February 2, 1880.*

from papers I discovered on Academia.edu and Jstor. org, the Kreitzberg Library at Norwich University (of all places), the Centre for Ottoman Studies, and letters buried deep in the archives of Constantinople University, found and translated by another dear friend, the renowned scholar Mehmet Lüle.

And this without leaving the sunny spot in our kitchen where I like to write. All in all, an extremely *satisficing* outcome. The story cleared up another mystery that has puzzled members of the family for generations: the origins of the 12-carat Imperial Red Topaz that my mother left to my sister, Brenda. She, being the more sensible sibling, has it safely secured in a bank vault in Melbourne.

Unlike the other stories in the series, I had no firsthand account, and so I've had to use my imagination more than I normally do with certain aspects of David's odyssey from Baghdad to Rhodes and back. So, while some of David Smulian-Hasson's actions may be contentious, rest assured: all the characters and events are accurate. Until, of course, proven otherwise.

THE GOLEM

Prologue *The Island of Rhodes, February 1840*

"*A*re you sure this is one of the men?" asked the sergeant. "The man you saw with the boy?"

"It is him. I am certain," replied the old woman, pointing a bony finger at the manacled man who stood trembling in the front office of the police station. "In any case, they all look alike. Vile creatures."

"Very well," said the sergeant to the two policemen who held the prisoner, "take Istamboli the Jew and put him in a cell while I send word to the governor."

For two days, the terrified and now-starving man—for he'd been given no more than a crust of bread and a cup of water since his arrest—lay in the small cell, wondering of what crime he was accused. On the afternoon of the second day, his question was answered, though the answer confused him even more.

"Murderer!" shrieked some of the villagers as the small contingent of gendarmes led the stumbling Istamboli through the streets of Rhodes City towards the governor's mansion.

One even threw a rock, which, fortunately for Istamboli, missed his head but knocked the fez off one of his guards.

The room into which Istamboli was dragged was crowded with people, all of them talking at Yusuf Pasha, Governor of Rhodes. Of course, Istamboli didn't recognize anyone, but he knew they were important. The group consisted of the kadi (or chief judge); the Greek Archbishop and his primates; and the consuls of Austria, Britain, France, Sweden, and Prussia. All had been invited by Yusuf Pasha to attend the interrogation.

"You," said Yusuf Pasha, pointing a long finger at Istamboli, who was by now so weak and terrified that he could barely stand, "are accused of killing a young Greek Christian boy on the afternoon of February 17th to use his blood in one of your mysterious rituals. Do you confess?"

For a moment, Istamboli thought he'd misheard the governor's accusation. But when the governor repeated the question about confessing, he managed to let out a heart-wrenching whimper, which the governor took as a "no."

"So," he repeated, "you deny the charge?"

"Yes, Your Excellency. I was in Lindos on that date with my friends." His voice was cracked and barely audible, and the governor asked him to repeat what he'd said. Once he was satisfied with the answer, the governor turned to the kadi.

"Have you been able to establish his alibi?"

"Not yet, Excellency, as these 'friends' have not been identified. It is my belief that we should hold him until we can find them to confirm or deny his alibi."

Before the governor could respond, Wilkinson, the British consul, slammed his fist on the table around which the other Europeans had gathered.

"Good God, man," said Wilkinson, "we are wasting time. One look at this wretch and you can tell he's lying."

The other European consuls murmured their agreement. "We insist you interrogate him as harshly as he deserves."

The governor looked uncertain for the moment. The kadi shook his head, and the European consuls hemmed and huffed impatiently. It was not a good idea, the governor thought, to antagonize the European representatives.

"Very well," he said, holding up his hand to silence the kadi, who was about to protest. "Let him be bastinadoed to see if it changes his mind."

Istamboli was thrown to the ground, and his bare feet were tied to a wooden pole held by two policemen. A third began to lash the soles of his feet with a thin cane. The torture lasted for twenty minutes. Istamboli passed out several times, and cold water was thrown on him till he regained consciousness. After five hundred lashes, the governor ordered the policeman to stop, and when Istamboli had recovered sufficiently to speak, the governor once again asked him to confess.

"To what?" Istamboli asked through a haze of pain and horror.

"Filthy Jew!" yelled the French consul. "Apply further torture."

A heavy weight was placed on Istamboli's chest and hot wires passed through his nose until the governor finally signaled for the torture to cease. Istamboli was placed in a chair (his feet were too swollen and damaged for him to stand) and told that the next round of torture would surely kill him. It was at that point that Istamboli—mad with pain—finally confessed to the murder, named his co-conspirators, and said *that they had taken the dead boy to the chief rabbi so that his blood could be used for making matzos.*

Shortly afterwards, the chief rabbi and nine elders of the Rhodes Jewish community were arrested and put to the torture. The Jewish quarter was surrounded by soldiers, and no food or water was allowed in for twelve days. Many young Greeks, including Wilkinson's own son, roamed the Jewish quarter, beating and even killing those who were too weak from hunger to fight back.

"Your Excellency," said the kadi when Yusuf Pasha granted him an audience. "It is my belief that you have committed a grave injustice against the Jews. You extracted a confession under duress, which the man Istamboli has since recanted. With the rabbi and other elders, you have used torture as a punishment. All of these have been outlawed by the Sublime Porte in Constantinople. The new Tanzimat laws are very clear in this regard."

"This is Rhodes," replied the pasha with a dismissive wave. "We are a speck in the great Ottoman Empire. Those laws don't apply here. In any case, the European consuls demanded it. What choice did I have?"

"You are in charge, effendi. I very much doubt that if word should reach Constantinople, the Europeans would shoulder any of the blame. There is no evidence that the crime in question was even committed. There is no body, and anyone with any knowledge of Jewish law knows that blood is never used in anything to do with food. This will not end well for you . . . or any of us."

In that he was right. What the *kadi* didn't know was the true motive behind the consuls' demands.

Chapter 1

Being bitten by a camel on the right cheek of his buttocks was not part of the plan. Not that there'd been much of a plan to begin with. All Ali Riza Pasha, Governor of Baghdad, had ordered David to do was kill Sayyid Ibrahim Za'farani, the dreaded gang leader of the city of Karbala, and his master, the powerful zealot who employed the jumped-up middle-class gangster.

"And who might Za'farani's employer be, Your Excellency?" asked David Smulian-Hasson, who, one week before the camel attack, sat across from the pasha in his elaborately furnished office in the governor's palace in Baghdad.

"I am about to tell you that," said the pasha, drumming his chubby fingers on his desk in irritation. He looked up at the man who sat opposite him with his thick black curls and soft smiling eyes and wondered, not for the first time, how such an innocent-looking person could be such an accomplished assassin. "My spies in Karbala suggest that Za'farani has lately become a disciple of Shaykh Kazim Rashti."

"But he is a respected leader of the Shiites, Your Excellency. Surely, he would not support a known gangster?"

"That is where you are wrong. I myself am a Shiite, and it pains me greatly to order action against one of my own sect." He picked up a pastry from a tray in front of him and popped it in his mouth. "But I cannot allow the gangs in Karbala to rule the city. Their everyday activities—murdering, embezzling, raping—those I could overlook, but the outrageous amount of money they extract from pilgrims heading to the shrine of Husayn ibn Ali, that I cannot ignore."

David was about to ask why the other crimes were less outrageous, but his attempt was cut off by the pasha, who stood up and walked to the window.

"It's a most holy shrine," the pasha continued. "Important to Muslims in all of Iraq, Iran, and as far away as India. Do you know the Nawab of Oudh is a supporter of the shrine?"

"That piece of information had escaped me, Excellency."

"Well, he is, and we don't need his contribution to dry up because of the behavior of those rogues. Now, can you do the job or not?"

This was not the first assassination commissioned by Ali Riza Pasha. All had required stealth and planning to ensure that nothing could be traced back to the Ottoman officials, and so far, David Smulian-Hasson had performed each task admirably. A corrupt magistrate who'd threatened to expose important officials had vanished before he could come to trial. The body of a retired Mamluk general whose record of atrocities could not be overlooked nor brought before the public was found in a dark alley, the victim of brigands. The spy who'd stolen state secrets and was about to pass them on to Aqasi—the grand vizier for Mohammad Shah Qajar, ruler of Iran—had been fished out of the Tigris twenty miles downstream. The assassinations had been handled efficiently and professionally, and the whole process had been painless for the pasha, though not for the victims.

"As always, Your Excellency," said David, standing up and putting his right hand over his heart, "it shall be done."

"But," replied the pasha, hearing the hesitation in David's voice, "I suppose you're going to tell me the fee is double if you're going to have to take out both parties."

"Actually," replied David, who had intended to do exactly that but made a snap decision to surprise the pasha, "I was going to say I will do both for the price of one. You've been a good customer."

Ali Riza laughed till the rolls of fat around his face and neck wobbled. "You never cease to amaze me, Smulian-Hasson. Two for the price of one, eh? What a brilliant idea. Nevertheless, if there is the slightest doubt that Rashti does indeed control Za'farani, then hesitate before you plunge in your *sica*. Having him alive would help me with future negotiations in the city. So, bear that in mind. But in the end, you must do what must be done. There is a delegation of clerics and officials leaving for Karbala tomorrow from the Bab Al-Talsim gate to meet with the Sayyid family, who are also opposed to the gangs. You can travel with them. I'll tell the *boluk-bashi*[2] to expect you. Now off with you, and report back on completion."

David bowed to the pasha, who waved him off and began to rifle through a pile of papers on his desk.

An hour later, David sat in the kitchen of the house he and his family lived in above a carpet store in the predominantly Jewish area of Baghdad known as Shorjah. The store served as a front for David's real occupation, as it had for his father and grandfather. It would one day play the same role in the life of his son.

Ruth, his wife of nine years, was busy putting the finishing touches on their dinner. From the shrieks of laughter coming from downstairs, his eight-year-old son Elias and five-year-old daughter Rebecca were causing havoc, jumping on the pile of new carpets that had just arrived from India.

"Smells good," David said, taking a sip of arak.

"Why wouldn't it?" asked Ruth, sprinkling cinnamon into the copper pot that simmered on the charcoal. "It's

---

[2] *The Ottoman equivalent of a captain.*

your favorite: lamb meatballs stuffed with apricots and prunes on top of saffron rice. And not that I'm counting, but that's your second glass of arak."

"I know," David replied, giving a deep sigh and setting the empty glass on the table. "It's this next job. Normally, I can picture precisely how I'll do it. This one seems really complicated. Za'farani is a public figure, and I can't imagine he's ever alone. And the shaykh, well, he'll be even more difficult."

"You'll find a way as you always do," Ruth said, bending down to kiss him on the cheek. "Now call the children while I dish up."

David smiled as his wife took four earthenware bowls from a shelf and began to ladle out the meatballs and rice. She never ceased to amaze him with her dispassionate reaction to his assignments. Just before his marriage, his father, Solomon, had warned him that it would be difficult to reveal his true profession to his future wife. In that he was wrong; she'd been totally unfazed.

"You say your family has been doing it for hundreds of years? Then who am I to suggest a break with tradition? So long as no one gets hurt and the money's good," she'd said nonchalantly.

David had looked carefully at Ruth to see if she was joking. From her rather vacant expression, it was clear she wasn't. "The money's good," he replied, putting his hands on her shoulders, "but someone does get hurt."

"Well, as long as it's not you. I couldn't bear that." He'd drawn her closer and kissed her gently on the forehead and wondered if she was slightly dimwitted. She wasn't, and as the years went by, he realized that Ruth was concerned only about those things she could control. His secret profession wasn't one of them.

He'd fallen in love with Ruth from the moment he'd seen the slender young woman with hair the color of a raven shopping for linens at the Shorja market with her mother. Their introduction was arranged by his parents through the rabbi, and when he'd satisfied her mother that he was a worthy suitor, they'd courted and a year later married. It was a small wedding, and the only outsiders were members of the powerful and wealthy Sassoon family, distant relatives of Ruth's father who'd helped her and her mother after her father's untimely death. Unlike many arranged marriages where the male takes the dominant role, theirs was one of equals. Neither would have had it any other way.

The soldiers and clerics were assembled at the gate when David rode up on the horse he'd bought just a few months before.

"You've a fine young horse, effendi," said the captain, who introduced himself as *Boluk-bashi* Djemal Fidan.

"Thank you," said David, doing his best to look like a seasoned rider, although he didn't fool Fidan one bit. "He's highly spirited, that's for sure."

"Then hold on tight," laughed the captain. "The pasha has instructed me to make sure you get to Karbala in one piece."

"That's good to hear, *Boluk-bashi*," replied David. "I always feel better when I arrive in a place in that state."

The captain laughed again. "Well, we have some old men in our party, so we will travel slowly. I estimate we should be there by tomorrow night. There is a decent caravanserai about twenty-four miles from the gate where we will stop for the night. You may ride up here with me if that is your wish or amid our column with the clerics."

"It would be best if I were somewhat inconspicuous," said David, who was wearing traditional loose white clothing suitable for making a pilgrimage to a holy city, "for I must disappear once we arrive in Karbala, as I'm sure the pasha has advised you."

"Indeed, he has. Though I am unaware of the task he has set for you. So perhaps it is best that you stick close to me on the ride, for the clerics will talk amongst themselves as old men are wont to do."

The column, which consisted of three cavalry officers and seventeen troopers, rode ahead. The coaches of the clerics came behind with another six troopers in the rear. Not enough to deter a major attack, but no one expected any trouble along the road. Anyone engaged in mischief was already in the lawless city of Karbala.

On the second day, close to evening, they saw Karbala, with its marble mosques and towering, gold-domed minarets glistening in the late afternoon sun. The closer they got, the more crowded the road became with pilgrims on their way to visit the tomb of Abbas ibn Ali. Most of the pilgrims traveled on foot, but a few rode camels and horses. Like David, all wore white robes.

David pulled his horse up next to Captain Fidan. "I think, *Boluk-bashi*, that I will leave you here and melt into the ranks of the worshippers. If I can complete my task before you are done, I will wait to join your column on its way back to Baghdad. If not, I will make my own way."

"We leave on the morning of the fourth day from today. God willing, we will see you then," said the captain, touching his chest.

"Ma'a as-salama," replied David as he fell back from the column and vanished into the dust kicked up by the crowd streaming into Karbala, intent on getting to the holy site before dark. The entrance to the city was chaotic with the pilgrims, many of whom were ruffians demanding money to ensure swift passage to the tomb, pushing against the city's inhabitants as they went about their business. David turned down a narrow alley away from the crowd and continued till he came to a square with an inn and a stable.

After he'd paid what he considered a hefty sum for stabling his horse, he asked for a room at the inn and, once again, was charged what he felt was an astronomical price.

"Not to cast aspersions on your inn," he said to the innkeeper, "but your prices are more akin to those charged at a palace."

"I take no offence, effendi," replied the man, who introduced himself as Kristo, an Albanian from Permet. "The taxes we must pay to those who control this area of the city force my hand. I promise you, though, that the room is most comfortable, and the food made by my wife will satisfy your hunger."

"And who is it that controls this neighborhood that has such power over you, who seems to be an honest man?"

"That depends on what day it is. One week, we are under the 'protection' of the gang leader Salih, and the next, his mortal enemy, Za'farani. This day, it is Za'farani who needs the money to recruit soldiers now that many of his men, members of his mother's tribe, are reputed to have gone back to the desert."

"How fortunate," David said, stroking his beard. In truth, he could not have had better news. The evening before he left for Karbala, it was Ruth who'd suggested that he announce himself as a soldier of fortune looking to apply his trade to whoever asked his business. It had been a brilliant suggestion and further proof—not that he needed it—that his wife was far smarter than he.

"Why is that?" asked Kristo. "You are a soldier?"

"Indeed, I am. I'm a *bashi-bazouk*[3], lately returned from Syria and seeking employment."

"Clearly not a struggling one," said the innkeeper, giving him a strange look from beneath his bushy eyebrows, "judging by the size of your purse."

David gave a silent curse. He'd been stupid to agree to the price without haggling. "Well, I am a soldier of fortune. Sometimes I have a fortune, sometimes I don't. It just so happens that my last employer was quite generous, though the money will not last long at the prices you charge." He said the last part with a grin. He had no need

---

[3] *An Ottoman mercenary.*

to antagonize the owner of the inn. "Now, my good man, how do I contact this Za'farani?"

"There is a tavern, just behind the square—the only one, you cannot miss it—where some of Ibrahim Za'farani's followers gather to drink *boza* each evening. They will know."

David thanked Kristo, who showed him to his room, which, while small, was clean and neat. He lay on the bed and began to visualize the evening ahead, and then, because he hadn't slept much the night before as he camped with the soldiers outside the caravanserai where the clerics slept, he closed his eyes and slept for an hour.

It was dark when he awoke, but he could smell the aroma of spicy food coming from below. He put on a pair of voluminous white trousers, an embroidered shirt, and a red waistcoat. He attached a leather bandolier to the waistcoat, and in its numerous scabbards, he put an array of daggers. A close examination would have revealed that his *sica* was not amongst the bandolier blades but rather attached to his left ankle under well-used leather boots. He looked formidable if not fierce. His features were too soft to frighten anyone.

After an excellent dinner of *tava e kosit*—which the innkeeper's wife told him was a traditional Albanian dish of lamb, eggs, and yoghurt—he set out to meet the men who worked for Za'farani.

Chapter 2

The tavern was noisy and smelled of the unwashed bodies of working men and hooligans mingled with the pungent sweetness of the *mu'assel* bubbling *shishas*. It was not a place where the laws against alcohol and tobacco held sway.

David asked for arak and found an empty table at the back of the room where he could watch the crowd. It didn't take long to determine which of the men worked for Za'farani. They were the loudest and most boisterous and used their affiliation with the gang leader to firmly establish the pecking order of the patrons, shoving people from the best tables and demanding money for the sweet fermented drink known as *boza*.

"Are you certain you wouldn't rather order *boza*?" asked the waiter. "Some people in here might take offence to you drinking arak, which they see as the drink of the wealthy and indolent."

"No," replied David, leaning back in his chair as if he were offended by the question. "I don't like *boza*. It upsets my stomach, and too bad if it offends anyone. It's my money." He said the last part loudly enough for people at nearby tables to hear. It was a dangerous ploy because most of the men in the tavern looked as if they'd like any excuse to slit a stranger's throat, but it was a risk he had to take. If he were to get close to their leader, he'd need to prove himself as ruthless as Za'farani's most dangerous gang members. He sipped his arak slowly and scowled at whoever looked his way. It didn't take long before one lout at a nearby table came over.

"What's the matter?" he said, his hand on the curved dagger he wore in a scabbard attached to his belt. "*Boza* not good enough for you?"

"If it's good enough for the likes of you," replied David, "then I fear it's a little below my standards."

For a moment, the man looked shocked. Then his face split into a terrifying grin, and he flipped the table over, sending the earthen flask with David's arak flying. The reaction he got from David was not what he expected. Instead of cowering, David stood up slowly.

"You see, this is what I mean. You have no respect for a good drink. Now, while I straighten the table, go and get me another flask of arak."

This time, the lout didn't hesitate. He pulled his dagger from the scabbard and lunged at David. In a move that was too quick to comprehend for most onlookers who'd turned to watch their champion slit the stranger from his gut to his groin, David rolled forward and drove his fist into an area along the sciatic nerve of his assailant. It was the exact move that had been taught to generations of our family members for use in situations where killing was not called for. The man's scream of pain as he tumbled to the floor was cut short by a second blow to his thorax, which sent shock waves to his brainstem and caused his eyes to roll back in his head. He lay on the floor, unable to move or emit more than a gurgle.

The crowd of patrons who'd gathered around the two men, eager to watch the insolent stranger get what was coming, gave a collective gasp. A few of the Za'farani men knelt beside their fallen comrade while others gaped at the stranger with open mouths. One of the ruffians, taller than the rest and dressed slightly better in a long black robe with an impressive turban on his pockmarked face, moved to the front.

"Who are you?" he said. "You wear the dress of a common *bashi-bazouk*, yet you fight with a skill that eclipses your appearance. The man you have incapacitated is one of Ibrahim Za'farani's best captains."

"Indeed," replied David. He knew he'd be equally incapacitated if the men attacked him as a group but was doing his best to appear calm. "Then Za'farani, who I assume is an important man, may need a replacement captain."

For an instant, the man's black eyes flashed, and then he laughed. "He may well. And yes, he is an important man. Ibrahim is also my brother."

"In that case," David replied, "perhaps you can put in a good word for me. I am in need of employment."

"Come," said the man, stepping over the still-quivering body of David's incapacitated assailant, "join me for a glass or two of *boza* or arak if you prefer. If I like you and believe your story, I will take you to meet my brother."

"Where did you learn to fight like that?" asked the man, who said his name was Amir Za'farani, as they sat down to order their drinks.

"I learned it from my father but perfected it when I fought with the Nawab of Oudh," replied David, who'd never set foot outside of Iraq but remembered the pasha telling him that the Nawab of the Indian princely state was a big contributor to the shrine of Al-Abbas. "It served me well when I fought in Syria for the Ottomans against the Khedive of Egypt."

"An unsuccessful campaign, as I understand."

"For the Ottomans, perhaps, but not for me. I saved the life of one of the Ottoman generals, and he rewarded me handsomely. As I told the inn keeper, I am a soldier of fortune, and if there is money in it, I don't care which side wins." David was enjoying himself. Not one thing he'd said was true, and he knew that so long as he didn't overelaborate, he could keep going till Amir agreed to take him to meet his brother or the booze ran out. Fortunately, it was the former, and he managed to stagger back to the inn before he was overly inebriated to get some sleep before he met with Ibrahim Za'farani the next morning.

He'd learned one crucial piece from Amir: Ibrahim Za'farani took orders from no man. Not even the powerful Shaykh Kazim Rashti.

Chapter 3

The headquarters of the Za'farani gang was a large, yellow brick building with wooden balconies and stone arches. David and Amir and three of the Za'farani hooligans walked together from the tavern where David had drunk with the younger Za'farani brother the night before. The closer they got to the headquarters, the more armed men they encountered.

"These are our soldiers who make sure that Mirza Salih and his Baluchi mercenaries can't get close to my brother."

"They're well-armed, I see," David said, wondering just how he was going to get away with completing his mission.

"Yes, swords, daggers, and, of course, miquelet pistols and muskets. Only a fool would attempt anything untoward. But come, my brother is a busy man."

The interior of the mansion was filled with fine carpets and expensive furniture, which made David think that whatever Za'farani stole or embezzled, he kept enough for himself to live like a nobleman. A huge African with hands the size of a camel's head took David's bandoliers but fortunately didn't search him for concealed weapons and so missed the *sica* strapped to David's left ankle.

Ibrahim Za'farani was lounging on a cushion listening to an older man who, from the little David could hear, was reporting on the gang's current financial situation. Za'farani didn't acknowledge Amir or David, which gave David the perfect opportunity to examine him carefully. He looked to be in his early thirties and rather heavy for someone who had the reputation as a fierce fighter. Like Amir, his eyes were almost black, and even under his beard, David could see that his face was set in a permanent scowl. After a few minutes, he dismissed his accountant with a wave of his pudgy hand and rose to his feet. He was not as tall as his brother, nor as friendly.

"Amir tells me you are a formidable warrior. That you took down one of my best captains with a movement that my men say is reminiscent more of a *jinni*[4] than a man." His tone conveyed suspicion rather than praise. "Well, go on, show me this magical move so I can judge for myself."

"I'm afraid that is not possible, effendi," replied David. "It's not a move I can demonstrate. It must be provoked."

"Oh? Well, then, allow me to provide the provocation. Mustapha!" he yelled, summoning his huge bodyguard, who lumbered into the room.

"Yes, effendi," replied Mustapha. "What is it you wish?"

"I wish you to kill this upstart fellow. Slit his throat, crush his ribs, rip his head from his neck. Whatever pleases you. But don't make too much mess . . . go on, go on."

Mustapha took one look at his boss and another at David and withdrew a long butcher knife from the sash he

---

[4] *A supernatural being.*

wore around his waist. Then, with a roar, he reached out to where David stood as if to grab him. His monstrous hand clasped thin air as David dropped into a roll. There was a flash of movement, and the giant went down, clutching his leg and screaming before David's hand scrambled the nerves in his neck, sending the same shockwaves to his brainstem as had disabled David's assailant from the night before. The only reason for not using the *sica* was that its presence needed to be kept secret. David wanted it to stay that way until he was ready to kill Za'farani.

Ibrahim Za'farani said nothing. He looked at David, who'd pulled himself up into a standing position, and then down at his huge bodyguard, who stared back at him with glassy eyes. Then he kicked the prone man in the head and stepped over his body.

"Impressive," he said as if he didn't mean it. "Well, you will replace him as my new bodyguard. Follow me; I need to urinate."

For the next two days, David accompanied Za'farani everywhere he went. He stood behind him at meals, walked ahead of him in the street, knelt beside him in the mosque, and stood outside the door when Za'farani met with important men in his quarters. He was allowed to eat with Amir and one or two of the other senior members of the gang once he'd secured Za'farani's quarters, and he slept on a divan just outside the gang leader's door at night. He could have killed Za'farani once he'd gone to bed, but on both nights, there were too many other people in the house for him to have made a clean getaway.

On the third day, Ibrahim Za'farani took him aside. "This evening, I will visit with a certain woman of my acquaintance. You will accompany me, but you will keep the meeting to yourself on pain of death. I will inform Amir and the others that I will be locking myself in my room to pray and read the Koran, and that while I am doing it, I have given permission for you to take the evening off. You will go to the side of the house in the alley, just below where my quarters are, and I will join you there. And make sure you wear *mufti*[5] rather than that outfit, which would attract too much attention."

"If I may say so, effendi," David said, trying to look worried rather than excited at the prospect of getting the gang leader alone, "it seems to me to be a dangerous deception, one fraught with uncertainty should something befall us. How will Amir and the others know if we are in trouble?"

"First," replied Za'farani, "you may not say so. It is not for you to question my actions. Second, my followers, including my brother, believe me to be a pious man who would never indulge in sexual acts outside of marriage, and I would like it to remain so. Third, it is your job to keep me safe. If you feel you are not capable, then I have no need of your services."

David gave a deep bow. "Fear not, effendi, I will allow no harm to befall you." Za'farani missed the flare of David's nostrils, a habit his wife knew indicated he was lying.

---

[5] *Ordinary clothing.*

David wished Amir and the other senior gang members a good night after getting a few tips on taverns and markets to visit. A few minutes later, he donned his white robes and met Ibrahim Za'farani, who'd climbed down a rope from his window eight feet above the alley.

"How will you get back in, effendi?" David asked. "That rope looks easier to climb down than up."

"Very simply," said Za'farani. "You will lift me up on your shoulders like Mustapha used to do before you incapacitated him."

"I hope I am up to the task," said David, now certain he'd have to kill Za'farani before he attempted to reenter his bedroom. There was no way he could lift the pudgy gang leader on his shoulders.

"You'd better be," said Za'farani, pulling his hood from the heavy cloak he wore over his head so that his face was in shadow. "Now follow me, but keep your eyes open for any of Mirza Salih's Baluchis. If they see me, we are both as good as dead."

Well, one of us will certainly be dead, thought David. *But it won't be me.*

They made their way out of the alley and then turned right onto a busy shopping street. The night was filled with the chatter and yelling of stall keepers and shoppers, and the grunts of camels waiting patiently for their owners to load them up before heading home. Most of the tradespeople looked ready to close their stalls but held off as customers made last-minute purchases for the evening meal.

It was a moonless night and quite dark save for the light from the oil lamps in the stalls and houses that danced across the shadows. To David's surprise, Za'farani was more friendly and talkative than he'd been inside his headquarters. He asked David about his family and sympathized when David told him that he'd grown up an orphan. He talked about his own family and how worried he was about Amir, who he thought lacked ambition.

David heard no more than half of what Za'farani said, so occupied was his mind with the thought of when and where he'd attempt to kill the gang leader. His musings were interrupted by a large group of men who walked with a swagger that conveyed both the arrogance of youth and the abusive nature of unbridled power. The men laughed and joked as they knocked into pedestrians and helped themselves to whatever took their fancy from the stalls, whose owners stood by with glum and resigned expressions on their faces.

Za'farani put his arm on David's. "Wait, these are Salih's men. Quick, into this courtyard." The entrance to the courtyard was between the stalls of a date seller and a knife sharpener. It was black as pitch, and at first it seemed as if they were the only occupants. Then they heard the deep belly-grunt of a camel that was upset at having its space invaded. Za'farani swatted at it, and it became even more agitated.

"Shut the beast up," whispered Za'farani. "Those Salih dogs will come to see what the commotion is."

"I have no idea how to do that," David whispered back.

"What are you, an imbecile?" asked Za'farani. "I pay you to know those things."

"Of camels I know very little," replied David, taking the *sica* from its scabbard and plunging it into the right kidney of Ibrahim Za'farani, who looked at David in disbelief. He made a sound very similar to that of the camel as he fell to the ground.

"Of death, though, I am a scholar," David said, bending down to wipe the blood from the *sica* with Za'farani's cloak.

And that's when the camel bit David on his right buttock. The roar David let out was at a higher pitch than Za'farani's death rattle or the agitated camel's grunts.

The noise in the street stopped, and within seconds, several curious Baluchis appeared at the entrance to the courtyard. In reality, the bite had been more surprising than painful, and as the men approached cautiously with daggers drawn, David made a call which no doubt saved his life: He pulled back the cowl that covered Za'farani's lolling head and yelled, "Death to the enemies of Mirza Salih!"

The Baluchis, still displaying wariness, moved forward till they could see Za'farani's body for themselves.

"By the Prophet's tooth," one of them said, "this man has killed Ibrahim Za'farani."

If David was expecting accolades, he was sadly disappointed. Instead of rushing forward to give him a pat on the back, the men looked confused and began to pull away. One of them turned to him.

"You think you have done a good thing for our boss, Mirza Salih?"

"Yes," said David, beginning to worry he'd made a dreadful mistake. "That was the idea."

"It was not a good one," replied the man. "Za'farani's soldiers outnumber ours. If they believe we are responsible for his death, there will be a war in Karbala that even the Turkish pasha in Baghdad cannot stop."

"Let's just kill him now, hand over his body, and tell them Za'farani's death was the work of this thief," said one of the thugs, waiving a nasty-looking knife at David.

"Hold on," shouted David, wondering how many of the Baluchis he could take out before he was killed. "That won't work. Za'farani's lieutenants are familiar with me. They'll know you're lying."

"He's right. If they know him, they won't believe he's a thief."

"Perhaps we should just hand him over to Amir Za'farani," said another of the men. "We can say we apprehended him in the act."

"That won't work either," said David. "I'll just tell them that Salih put me up to it."

"Not if we cut out your tongue," said another one of the Baluchis, brandishing his equally nasty-looking blade.

"I'll still have these," said David, holding up his hands. "I can write. However, before you think too hard on the situation, I'd like to propose an alternative solution."

"What is it?" asked the man with the knife.

"We—or rather you—get rid of his body, and I vanish from the city. That way, they may think he's been kidnapped."

"Someone will see us carrying his body."

"Not if you put his arms around the shoulders of your biggest men and carry him along as if he were drunk. Dump him in the desert for the vultures or whatever you do with the bodies of the people you kill. Hardened soldiers like yourselves have done it before."

The Baluchis closed ranks and began to discuss David's proposal. Then, having weighed up the pros and cons, they turned back to him, or at least to where they'd last seen him. To their surprise, David had vanished. They gave a collective yell and, grabbing Za'farani's body, rushed back onto the street.

David waited in the shadows behind the camel, hoping the beast wouldn't bite him again. After what he felt was sufficient time for the gang to disperse, he stepped from the courtyard onto a now-empty street and made his way to the stable, where he retrieved his horse and rode to the city gate to wait for Captain Fidan and his party. They appeared shortly after dawn.

"As-salaam 'alykum, *Boluk-bashi*," said David.

"Wa alaikum assalam," replied the captain with a smile. "It is barely light, and the city is already abuzz with the news that Za'farani has vanished. Last seen in the company of his bodyguard, a terrifying-looking *bashi-bazouk*. That could never be you. No one would mistake you for terrifying."

David shook his head and smiled. "Well, then, this is as good a time as any to leave this place. The people were not to my liking."

"One in particular, I imagine," laughed the captain. "Now, let's ride so we can be away from here before total chaos ensues."

Chapter 4

"Everything went well?" asked Ruth when David appeared in the carpet store the next afternoon.

He wrapped her in his arms and kissed her gently. "Just as you said it would, my love."

"The problem with you is that you worry about everything. You worry about me and the children, and yet we are all fine and healthy. You worry about doing your job, and yet you are gifted by God."

"I'm not sure God is involved. This gift, as you call it, is an alleged curse put on my family by the Levites eighteen hundred years ago when my ancestors were still running around the Judean Desert in sheepskin underwear, breaking the Ten Commandments at every opportunity."

She patted his face. "I don't believe in curses."

"And I don't believe in God," he replied with a mischievous grin, knowing she'd be upset.

But she'd known him too long and so knew what he was up to. "That's why you worry—because you know you are committing terrible acts of blasphemy."

"As long as you don't tell the rabbi, I'll be OK."

"And as long as you stick to blasphemy and not coveting thy neighbor's wife, I won't. Now go up and get the children ready for dinner."

Just after dinner, when David and Ruth had put the children to bed, a messenger arrived from the governor of Baghdad.

"His Excellency, Ali Riza Pasha, requests you attend him at noon tomorrow. He wished me to say expressly that you should not worry."

"You see," said Ruth, "even the pasha himself knows you to be a worrier."

"My father told me that in our profession, only those who worry survive. Especially when it comes to dealing with an Ottoman pasha. Remember how his predecessor, Dawud Pasha, treated us . . . driving the great Sassoon and Judah families out of Iraq to India in fear of their lives."

"Of course, and I understand. As you know well, David Sassoon was my protector. But, my darling, try to lighten up a little when we are all together. I don't want our children thinking that their father broods constantly."

David took exception to that. He didn't feel particularly somber, especially when he was with his children. But he knew enough not to argue with his wife, whom he loved more than life itself, as she never lost an argument.

"I'm sure all he wants to do is discuss payment and tell you what a good job you did," Ruth said as she blew out the oil lamp.

She was correct in both instances. The pasha was pleased with the way things had gone down in Karbala and thought David's fee was outrageous. There was, however, a third matter that he wanted to discuss, an assignment so secret that even he wasn't privy to the details.

At a little after noon the next day, David was escorted to the same office where Ali Riza Pasha had given him the assignment just over a week before. The pasha was drinking coffee and eating pastries, which had left crumbs all over his cluttered desk.

"Ah, my friend the assassin. It appears that you fulfilled the assignment in a most satisfactory way. Shaykh Kazim Rashti has distanced himself from the remnants of the Za'farani gang and, together with the Sayyad family, wishes to discuss how together we can move Karbala from being a wild and lawless town to a peaceful Ottoman city."

David inclined his head. "My thanks, Your Excellency. I am honored to have served you well, as I will again if a humble man like myself should be lucky to earn further assignments."

"You're not good at groveling, David Smulian-Hasson," said the pasha, trying to look grim but failing. "Come, come, man. We've known each other for a few years now, and both of us know secrets about each other."

"You are correct, Excellency, but I am but a lowly carpet salesman who is ignorant of anything concerning a grandee such as yourself." David said this with a subtle smile, and the governor laughed out loud.

"If you're going to lie, Master Assassin, try to control your nostrils. Your fee, by the way, is obscene, but...." He picked up a heavy purse from his desk and tossed it to David. "I am in a good mood and not about to quibble. In any case, you'll need the money to travel."

"To travel, Excellency?"

"Yes, to travel. You heard me. I have orders for you from Mustafa Reşid Pasha, Foreign Minister of the Ottoman Empire and advisor to the newly crowned Sultan Abdülmecid. You are to proceed to Constantinople immediately."

David was stunned. What in God's name could the foreign minister want with him?

"In case you expect me to reveal what it is they expect from you, I am equally in the dark."

"Surely it must be a mistake," said David, trying to catch his breath.

"No, this is genuine." The governor wiped some crumbs off a thick piece of parchment and handed it to David. "There is no mistaking Reşid Pasha's seal. You are to travel as fast as is possible from here to Constantinople, where you will be given an undisclosed assignment from the sultan himself."

"I am in shock, Excellency," David said, looking at the seal on the paper. It was written in Ottoman Turkish, which he both spoke and understood.

"Well, don't be. You will leave tomorrow in the company of soldiers bound for Constantinople. It is not a short journey, but you should reach there within the month."

"Your Excellency, I need a day or two to make provision for my wife and children."

"I will see that they lack nothing in your absence." He wrote a note on a piece of paper and handed it to David. "Give this to my assistant. It instructs him to check on your wife every week while you are away and to provide for your family. There is no need for concern. Now, off you go, and don't reveal a word of this to anyone. You can brief me on your return. Good luck, my friend."

Ruth took the news a lot more calmly than David. "You should take this as a great honor. Obviously, the foreign minister has a task he wishes you to perform."

"Yes, but why me?"

"Because you are the best. Now close your mouth because I know you're going to tell me that you are worried about me and the children. First, the pasha has said he will ensure we are taken care of. Second, we have more than enough money saved to last us three years, let alone three months. Third, we may not still have our parents, but we have neighbors and friends. All will be fine. Come, I'll help you pack, although I'm not sure you have clothes fine enough for a palace."

David did not sleep well that night. Despite Ruth's admonition, he was worried. His concern was not about his family, as he knew they'd be taken care of, or even what the sultan wanted of him. The thing that really made the hair on the back of his neck stand up was how the foreign minister knew of his occupation.

He would have been even more concerned if he'd known that a month later, a man would visit his store and speak to his wife about engaging him in a very special assignment. But he didn't hear about that until much later.

Chapter 5

Sir Moses Montefiore, President of the Board of Deputies of British Jews, was not pleased with Adolphe Crémieux, Vice President of the Consistoire Central des Israélites de France. In truth, he despised the little man. If asked why, and no one ever had, the Italian-born British baronet would have had a hard time pinpointing the precise reason he loathed his French colleague. There was just something about the little lawyer's constant liberal espousing that annoyed the hell out of him.

At that moment, they were sitting in a room in the Topkapi Palace waiting for Mustafa Reşid Pasha, foreign minister to the seventeen-year-old sultan of the Ottoman Empire, to arrive and escort them into the presence of His Highness Sultan Abdülmecid I.

"Listen, Crémieux, we cannot afford for any tension that exists between us to be observed by the foreign minister or the sultan," said Sir Moses as quietly as he could. It was not easy for the six-foot-three banker to keep his voice low.

Crémieux, a much smaller man whose face was permanently scrunched, drew his brows together as if he were about to pass wind. Then he took a breath and nodded his head.

"My apologies, Sir Moses. I am as determined as you to exact revenge on those who have visited such atrocities on our brethren in Rhodes and Damascus. I realize that because of my country's lack of funding for this mission—"

"—and lack of support," said Sir Moses.

"Yes, and lack of support . . . I am in a less-elevated position than you, who has the backing of my Lord Palmerston himself, but my heart and brain are as heavy as yours when it comes to how the Jews have been foully treated by those swine."

"I do not question your passion, Adolphe, believe me. The good news is that we have effected the release of the Jews rotting in prison from the authorities and had the rights of those who were subject to such terrible discrimination and falsehoods restored. We have established their innocence, which has been accepted by the Ottoman and Egyptian authorities. Their liberation is complete. And while I took the lead, your help was invaluable."

The little lawyer—who'd once presented a petition to Napoleon Bonaparte, discussed weight measure with the new French king, and filled courtrooms with his brilliant and biting oratory—was not intimidated by Sir Moses.

"Your generosity, Sir Moses, is exceeded only by your humility."

His sarcasm failed to penetrate the worry-filled haze that enveloped his colleague. Sir Moses blinked.

"Ah, yes. Well, now it is simply a matter of discussing

how we will get revenge. You have the name of the person recommended by David Sassoon in Bombay, do you not?"

"I'd be a fool to go into the presence of the sultan if I didn't," Crémieux snorted, his patience wearing thin. "This is why sometimes you find me disagreeable. It is questions like that, where you treat me as an imbecile, that raise my ire."

Their interaction was interrupted by the arrival of Reşid Pasha, resplendent in a navy-blue stambouline with gold piping.

"Welcome to the Sublime Porte, my friends," he said, clasping first Crémieux's hand and then that of Sir Moses. He was closer in age to Crémieux than he was to Sir Moses but more akin to the Englishman in his demeanor, which surprised neither Montefiore nor Crémieux.

Mustafa Reşid Pasha the Great had served as ambassador to both France and the United Kingdom and was considered one of the greatest statesmen of his time. He was also a terrible snob who would, under normal circumstances, have thumbed his nose at members of the Hebrew race. This time, however, restraint was called for as both were connected to some of the most powerful people in Europe.

He gave his guests his broadest smile. "His Highness is most appreciative that you've delayed your journeys home to come to Constantinople."

"It is I . . . uh, it is we who are honored to be seen by His Highness," said Sir Moses. "The speed at which he has addressed the hardships of his Jewish subjects has been nothing short of miraculous."

"And the imprint of your own hand, Excellency," interjected Crémieux, "is clear."

The pasha smiled. "My dear Crémieux, you have always been most perceptive, and I appreciate your recognizing my small part in this whole sad affair."

Crémieux gave Sir Moses a sneer, and the Englishman glowered in return. "Of course, I see your involvement, too, Pasha. I was simply waiting to thank you at a more appropriate time."

Reşid Pasha waved him off and then moved closer to the two men. "You realize that what we shall discuss with the padishah cannot be known by anyone else. No one in either of your governments. Not your colleagues. Not even your wives, who I know have accompanied you on this trip."

"You have my word," Sir Moses said, placing his hand over his heart. He looked at Crémieux, who'd raised his eyebrows.

"Naturally, my dear Pasha, it goes without saying," said the Frenchman. "The delicate nature of our discussion and the subsequent operation would be tantamount to treason in my country."

"And mine," Sir Moses said.

"Very well," Reşid Pasha said, nodding his head. "Then let us proceed. Follow me if you please." The Pasha led them down a long corridor till they came to a pair of huge wooden doors guarded by two soldiers. The guards stepped aside, and the pasha ushered them into the sultan's study.

Both visitors knew the thirty-first sultan of the Ottoman Empire was young, but the thin boy with the beginnings of a moustache who sat—or, more accurately, slumped—in the chair behind a desk stacked with papers took them by surprise.

"My Padishah," said Reşid Pasha, giving the sultan a low bow, "may I present Sir Moses Montefiore and Monsieur Adolphe Crémieux, the two Jewish leaders of whom we spoke."

"Ah, yes," said the sultan, rising from his desk and walking over to the visitors, who both inclined their heads. Abdülmecid extended a bony hand that at first confused his visitors as to his intentions. Then Crémieux shook it carefully, and the sultan gave him the hint of a smile. Sir Moses followed with a firmer handshake that caused the sultan to wince.

"I am trying to introduce more of the customs of Europe into my court," the sultan said, returning to his seat. "The handshake is one of them, though I'd prefer not to have my hand squeezed quite so violently."

"My sincere apologies, Your Highness," said Sir Moses, giving a deep bow.

"No matter," said the sultan, tapping his fingers on his desk as if to see if his hand was still operable. "It is something I suppose I must get used to if I am to meet other European leaders."

Rẹsid Pasha inclined his head. "My Padishah will have much to teach European leaders, too."

"You think so?" asked the sultan with the expression of a schoolboy who has just found a forgotten bun in his pocket.

"I know so, my Padishah. But we must get to the business you wish to discuss with our distinguished visitors quickly because your schedule is full for the day."

"Perhaps so, but I am the sultan, and if I run late with meetings, then who is anyone to question me?"

"No one would dare," responded the pasha.

"But you are right, my dear Mustafa. I am keen to know the identity of this man whose talents are so prodigious that these gentlemen have traveled so far to enlighten me. Please sit, my good sirs, and tell me about him so that I might judge if he is suitable for the assignment."

"Thank you, Your Highness. We know you have done so much to right the wrongs that were visited upon our community in Rhodes and Damascus. All European Jews will be eternally grateful for your assistance."

"Yes, yes, Sir Moses," said the sultan, who even at seventeen knew groveling when he heard it. "No need to go into that. You are aware that I issued a *firman*[6] denouncing the blood libels of Rhodes and Damascus?"

"All Jews are grateful for that, Your Highness," said Sir Moses, trying to sound less humble than before.

---

[6] *Decree.*

"I should hope so," said the sultan. "But for now, I am more interested in the final phase of this unpleasant situation. I want those who instigate mischief in my empire to pay for their arrogant disregard of my edicts. Now, you say you have the man who can ensure it happens?"

"We do, Your Highness," said Crémieux. "His name is David Smulian-Hasson, and he resides in one of the other great cities of your empire: Baghdad."

"Excellent," said the sultan. "I would prefer the job to be undertaken by one of my subjects. Neither of you is from that part of the world, so how is it you know of him?"

"His name was given to us by David Sassoon, who was once treasurer in Baghdad until he was driven out by Dawud Pasha, Your Highness," said Sir Moses.

"Yes, Dawud Pasha. A nasty and avaricious man, as I heard my father describe him. I believe he was dismissed."

"He was, my Padishah," said Reşid Pasha, who'd remained standing the whole time, pacing back and forth as if he were in a hurry for the meeting to be over. "He is now a custodian of the shrine at Medina, where he can do no more harm to the integrity of the empire. David Sassoon is one of the most successful merchants in all of India, and he had occasion to employ this David Smulian-Hasson and his father before him on several occasions."

"So," said the sultan, "you believe him to be accomplished at his profession?"

"According to David Sassoon, he is a master assassin," said Crémieux. "It is said his family have been assassins for nearly two thousand years using a mystical dagger called a *sica*."

"How interesting. I should like to see this *sica*," said the sultan, raising his eyebrows. "So, you believe he is capable of carrying out the task I shall set for him?"

"More than capable, Your Highness," said Sir Moses.

Reşid Pasha walked over to the sultan and put a letter in front of him. "As a precaution, my Padishah, I took the liberty of consulting with Ali Riza Pasha, your governor of Baghdad, who too has had occasion to utilize the services of this Smulian-Hasson. As you can read, he is most praiseworthy of the fellow and believes him to be of the utmost discretion."

"Very well," said the sultan, "send for him immediately. I shall question and brief him myself. Thank you, gentlemen, for making the trip. Your faith in this David Smulian-Hasson fills me with confidence. Hopefully, what happens next will justify your travels. Now, if you will excuse me." He looked down at his desk and began to read a paper while Reşid Pasha ushered the two Europeans from the room.

"You may believe you came a long way for what could have been accomplished in a letter," said Reşid Pasha when the guards had closed the doors leading to the sultan's office. "I assure you that is not the case. Your very presence has reassured the sultan, who, like all young men, can be fickle at times."

"We understand," said Sir Moses, "and the fact that we came underlies our belief in the importance of what is to happen."

"Excellent," said Reşid Pasha, giving him and Crémieux a pat on the back. "Then why don't you stay for a few days as my guests, and I will arrange for you to experience the beauty and mysteries of Constantinople."

Both Sir Moses Montefiore and Adolphe Crémieux and their wives stayed in Constantinople for a week before returning to Europe. The discussion that took place during their meeting with Sultan Abdülmecid remained a secret (until now, that is), but their triumphant return to Europe, where they were credited with obtaining the release of the Jews of Rhodes and Damascus, was celebrated by their fellow Jews and praised by a number of politicians including Prince von Metternich of Austria and Britain's Prime Minister William Lamb.

Chapter 6

The caravan journey from Baghdad to Alexandretta had taken David and the company of soldiers commanded by *Boluk-bashi* Fidan, the same man who'd escorted David to Karbala and back, just under three weeks. The journey had been neither easy nor pleasant. The Battle of Nezib—in which Ibrahim Pasha, son of Muhammad Ali, the powerful Khedive of Egypt, had defeated the Ottoman forces—had taken place less than a year before, and the countryside still crawled with deserters and bandits preying on travelers. It would not be long before the Khedive would acquiesce to European pressure and accept the hereditary rule of Egypt on condition that he withdraw his forces from Syria. But at that moment, the Ottomans had not yet reestablished themselves, which left the territory lawless at best and downright dangerous at worst. The twelve heavily armed cavalrymen (and one less-heavily-armed assassin) under Captain Fidan came under fire no more than ten miles from Aleppo.

The attack came just as the *boluk-bashi* called a halt for the day. It had been a hard ride, and the men were only too happy to set up camp close to a rocky outcrop. The lookout, who'd been posted just below the summit of the outcrop, gave the first part of a warning and then tumbled down over the rocks as a bullet took him in the left shoulder.

There were at least fifteen in the gang, a rag-tag collection of bandoliered men in long black robes and tightly wound turbans. A few carried long-barreled miquelet muskets, the same ones used by the troops, while others waved yatagans, the single-edged short saber of the Ottomans. They came out of the desert, hidden at first by a small dune and the glare of the setting sun. So terrifying were their demented screams and battle cries that they appeared to David more like demons than men, and were it not for the stern yet calm command of Captain Fidan, David believed the Ottoman troops would have turned and run. As it was, the troops had barely enough time to fire off one round from their muskets before the bandits were on them. How many died from that volley, David had no idea. He saw men flung backwards and others yell in pain, but still they came on in a cloud of dust and chaos.

Violence had always been part of his life, but that was one-on-one violence. This was different. All around him, men were yelling, snarling, screaming in agony. Captain Fidan shouted for David to stay back as his men, their muskets now useless, met the brigands with their sword bayonets. Two of the soldiers went down shrieking as the bandits' yatagans sliced open their bellies, spilling their entrails onto the sand. Captain Fidan fired his pistols, killing one of the bandits and shattering the arm of another. Then the leader—or the man David, in a moment of horror, thought was the leader, judging by the way he fought—ran right at him, his yatagan raised for a slashing stroke. He was a huge man with a scar that ran from his left eye to below his jaw, splitting his lips and exposing his rotting teeth in a ghoulish grimace.

For Captain Fidan, who'd turned in horror as he realized David's predicament, everything went into slow motion. He saw David drop to one knee and then tumble sideways as the bandit leader swung his yatagan. David's arm moved in a perfect arc, and the bandit leader arched his back and howled at the sky as David's *sica* severed his kidneys. Then David was up, whirling like a dervish as another of the bandits sprang at him and died. Whether it was the death of their leader or the sight of a man who appeared more *jinni* than human, the fight had gone out of the remaining bandits. Those who could turned and fled back across the dunes into the now-purple desert, leaving behind the bodies of seven of their comrades, plus two dead and one severely wounded soldier.

No one said a word to David, but they looked at him in a different way than they had before the skirmish. Captain Fidan ordered his men to bury the two soldiers and drag the dead bandits away from the camp to be disposed of by hyenas and carrion birds.

When they had eaten dinner—dried apricots, bulgur, and hardtack—Captain Fidan handed David a flask of arak.

"After Karbala, I knew you were a man of special skills," he said, giving his mustache a twist. "Now I have had the privilege to witness them firsthand. It is an honor to have seen you in action."

David took a sip of the arak and handed the flask back to the *boluk-bashi.* "No, Captain, it was my honor to see how you commanded your men under the circumstances. What I did is simply what I do."

The captain nodded his head and laughed. "Well, I didn't realize that selling carpets required such expertise with a blade, but we learn something new each day, as my father told me."

Chapter 7

In Alexandretta, they discovered that the entire Otto-man fleet had defected to the Khedive, and they had to settle for passage on a Lebanese trading ship. The voyage took them along the southern coast of Turkey, stopping at Antalya and Smyrna, through the Dardanelles Straits into the Sea of Marmara. It was almost five weeks to the day he'd kissed his wife and children goodbye when David finally saw Constantinople, the great capital of the Ottoman Empire.

The boat anchored in the calm waters of what Captain Fidan, who'd been to Constantinople before, told David was called the Golden Horn. To their right was Galata, with its shining minarets and domes and houses of all hues, and above it the mansions and palaces of Pera. But it was the opposite bank that took away whatever breath remained in David's lungs. Here was *the* Constantinople, spread out like a sleeping god on seven hills, each topped with a mosque, their gilded minarets sparkling in the late afternoon sun. Huge seraglios (including the Topkapi Palace, which was more magnificent than the rest) and tall towers and sparkling white houses interspersed with groves of trees and terraced gardens made up the most magnificent sight David had ever seen.

"Impressive, is it not?" asked Captain Fidan, who knew it was a question that no one other than a poet possessed the words to answer. David just shook his head, too overcome with emotion to speak. "You will spend the night in Pera at an inn, and I will send word to Reşid Pasha that you have arrived."

"What about you and your men?" asked David. He'd grown fond of the *boluk-bashi* over the course of the journey. Fidan had shared many things with David about his life as a soldier and a husband and father to three daughters, and he had enquired about David's life, though David's answers were more guarded. It was obvious that he knew David was not traveling to Constantinople to discuss recarpeting the sultan's palace, but if he suspected the real purpose, he kept it to himself.

"When I have seen you to the hotel—"

"I am unfamiliar with the word 'hotel,'" David interrupted.

"It is nothing but a fancy European word for an inn. I am told it is quite luxurious, certainly compared to where we have lain our heads this past month. As for me, I'll be staying in less salubrious quarters. My men and I will go to the military barracks to arrange our return to Baghdad. It has been a pleasure to travel with you, and I wish you luck with your mission, though I don't imagine luck plays much of a part in your life."

David laughed. "How much luck does a simple carpet salesman need? No, I'm afraid I can leave nothing to luck or providence. But I appreciate your wishes, for I know they come from the heart. Well, I wish you a safe journey back, and I shall look you up when I return to Baghdad, my friend, if I may call you that?"

"I should very much like that, Smulian-Hasson Effendi. Though I fear you will not be able to tell me much about your journey once you have seen Reşid Pasha."

The hotel was large and the lobby even more elegant than the governor's palace in Baghdad, with velvet-covered chairs, gold lamps, and large pots that overflowed with exotic plants. The owner, an Armenian in a western-style suit and red slippers, welcomed David with a glass of mint tea.

"I have been told to expect you, effendi, and to afford you the same courtesy I would with some of the foreign officials who frequent my establishment."

"And had you not been warned of my arrival, would you still afford me the same courtesy?" asked David.

"Of course not," replied the Armenian. "We are very particular about whom we allow in."

"Well, you're an honest man," replied David. "I appreciate that."

"I try to be. Talking of which, may I suggest you use our hammam? You have the look of someone who has not attended to his personal hygiene for some time."

David smiled. "Once again, your honesty does you credit. Yes, I have not had many opportunities to bathe since leaving Baghdad. I shall visit your hammam before I lay my foul body upon your clean sheets."

If the hotelier picked up the cynicism in David's tone, he ignored it. He summoned a servant to show David to the subterranean baths, where he was steamed and scrubbed and pummeled until he was free of the dust and dirt of the desert and the salt from the voyage.

He changed into clean white robes—not the fancier embroidered ones Ruth had packed for his meeting at the palace but those suitable for exploring a sophisticated city—and walked out to get a feel for Pera and Galata. It was late evening but still light and mild, and the streets were bustling with people of myriad ethnicities, many of whom David had only read about. There were Europeans in long frock coats and top hats going to and from the enormous embassy buildings of Pera. He recognized fellow Jews in black robes and Greeks wearing bright blue jackets over white kilts. Veiled women in sedan chairs carried by muscular porters competed for space with burly soldiers in black astrakhan hats and liveried footmen running alongside horse-drawn carriages. David watched in wonderment as the pageant of diversity that was the Ottoman Empire unfolded before him. Then his stomach growled, and he decided to look for food.

A large, cobbled square was filled with food vendors selling some dishes he recognized and others he didn't. He was not normally an adventurous eater—though he'd been forced to become one on the journey from Baghdad —so when he saw a stall selling lamb kebabs with chopped apricots and dates wrapped in bread that had just been taken out of a clay oven, he bought two. They were delicious, almost as good as Ruth's.

At that moment, any feeling of awe and amazement vanished as he thought of his family back in Baghdad. It had been over a month since he'd seen them, and who could say how long it would be before he did so again? It was the longest he'd ever been away, and the journey wasn't over yet. He wondered what Ruth was doing at this moment. She was most probably putting the children to bed, though he had no idea whether it was the same time in Baghdad as it was in Constantinople. On that somber note, he made his way back to the hotel and went to bed.

Chapter 8

David awoke at *Salat al-Fajr*, the first call to prayer that echoed from the minaret of the mosque nearby, but lay on his bed till well after sunrise, composing his thoughts for the day ahead. He had no inkling whether this was to be the day he'd be summoned, but it was good to be prepared just in case.

The hotel offered tea and coffee, and sweet pastries and flatbread with olive spread. Service was in the open courtyard. It was warm and sunny, and David was shown to a table toward the back, separated from some of the European guests by two large plant-filled copper urns. He was on his second pastry when the innkeeper approached his table. While his manner was slightly more deferential than it had been when David arrived, there was no mistaking the undertones of contemptuousness that oozed from every pore.

"You have an important visitor," he said.

"Show him to my table," David replied. "He can see for himself how you discriminate against citizens of the Ottoman Empire in favor of the Europeans."

The hotelier gasped. "That is a harsh accusation. I thought this table was shadier than the others. Well, be that as it may, your visitor requests that you meet him outside the hotel, where you will see a coach. He is inside."

David wondered whether he should go to his room and change into his fancier robes but decided he'd better check with whoever was in the carriage to see if this was indeed the day of his meeting with Reşid Pasha and the sultan.

The carriage was a shiny black brougham drawn by four horses. A driver in a black uniform sat on the elevated seat staring straight ahead as if his head were fixed in that position. There were no crests or markings on the carriage, which caused David to hesitate and doubt if this was actually the coach of a grandee. Then a high-pitched voice demanded he get in.

"Be quick," the driver said as David pulled himself in through the half-open door. "Time is of the essence, and the pasha does not wait upon the tardiness of others."

David fell back into the seat as the carriage began to move and found himself looking at the oddest person he'd ever seen. The man—at least he appeared to David to be a man—had a bald head that resembled a huge gourd covered in layers of fat so that his eyes were like two specks of charcoal in a cave of flesh. He wore a pale blue robe embroidered with gold circles beneath a darker blue cloak that clung to his obese body, and his pudgy hands were folded on his lap.

"Why do you stare at me with your mouth open as if you were waiting to trap a fly?" asked the man. "Have you never met a eunuch before?"

"Forgive me, Master Eunuch," David said, doing his best to sound deferential. "In truth, I have not, but I am extremely pleased to make your acquaintance. I am David Smulian-Hasson."

"Yes, yes, I am aware of who you are," the eunuch replied, flicking a finger in irritation. "I am Amrani Lahlou, chief assistant to the great Reşid Pasha, whom you will meet at the Topkapi. Now silence. There is nothing more for you to know."

"Um—" began David.

"I said you should be quiet."

"I only wanted to ask if my clothing is suitable for a meeting with such a distinguished man."

"There," said Amrani, flicking his finger towards a packet on the seat next to David. "That is for you to wear over your clothes. Put it on before we exit the coach at the water."

The packet contained a black robe with a hood that fitted over his small turban and made him look and feel like a sinister character out of a story meant to scare children. The carriage descended the steep cobbled street until it came to a small dock where a boat, manned by four burly rowers, waited to take them across the Golden Horn to the palace.

Amrani Lahlou was far more agile than his bulky appearance would seem to allow, and to David's surprise, he moved quickly from the carriage to the boat, where a low chair had been set up for him under an awning. There was no specific seating for David, who perched on a coil of rope as the boatmen rowed them across the water to another dock where a second carriage stood. As soon as they were seated, the driver walked around to each door and drew the curtains across the windows, blocking out light and fresh air.

"It's very hot in here," said David, who was beginning to sweat.

"The journey is a short one," replied the eunuch, "and the pasha desires your arrival at the palace to be a secret, or at least as inconspicuous as is possible, so cease your whining."

Ten minutes later, the coach stopped, and the door was opened by the coachman. When David's eyes got used to the light, he saw that they were in an alley next to a narrow door in a towering wall that he assumed led to somewhere in the palace. Lahlou tapped on the door with a fly whisk he produced from the sleeve of his robe. He did so three times, and the door was opened by a guard in a blue-and-gold braided jacket, who let them into what appeared to be a storeroom for old furniture.

"Keep your hood up," said the eunuch, "and follow me." He led David down a narrow stone passage to a set of stairs. "Climb to the very top and tap twice on the door. The pasha will let you in." With that, he turned and retreated down the passage toward the storeroom.

As David climbed the stairs, he began to feel anxious. The stairwell was narrow, and the only light came from an oil lamp at the first landing. He paused for a moment at the heavy wooden door, wondering if this was the top. Suddenly, a metal grate in the door slid open, and he saw a pair of eyes staring at him.

"Excuse me," he said, but the grate slammed shut. He stood for a few seconds and then saw a second set of stairs just off to his right. He knew nerves were not a good trait in his business, but he couldn't shake off the overall feeling that this whole affair would not end well. Another oil lamp hung on a hook on the second landing, and the blue door was less imposing than the one on the first landing. He held up his hand to knock, but the door opened before his knuckles made contact with the wood.

"It took you a while to climb a single flight of stairs," said the short man dressed in a dark blue stambouline and matching fez. "I am Mustafa Reşid Pasha, and you are?"

"David Smulian-Hasson, Your Excellency. I am the man you sent for."

"Of course I sent for you—otherwise you wouldn't be here. May God take your soul if your conversation is to be vapid in front of the sultan. Now come in, man, and make no sound until you reach my office."

David, gritting his teeth at the sheer cheek of the pompous little man, followed Reşid Pasha down a carpeted corridor whose walls glimmered in gold, blue, and white tiles until they came to an intricately carved wooden door, which opened into the office of the Foreign Minister for the Sublime Porte.

David's initial impression of Mustafa Reşid Pasha was echoed by many conservative officials in the Sublime Porte. Even the pasha's sobriquet, "The Great," spoke as much about his ego as it did his accomplishments. One of the most famous Turkish poets called Reşid an "apostle of civilization," and in an empire clinging like a drowning man to a floating branch on a primordial ocean of orthodoxy, he was without doubt a visionary. He'd had a lightning-fast rise through the ranks of officialdom, becoming ambassador to both France and Britain, and his involvement in the Tanzimat reforms (as acknowledged by both Crémieux and Montefiore) became the blueprint for the modernization of Turkish civil society. If anyone knew—and understood—the intrigues of the palace, it was most certainly he.

The pasha indicated a long leather couch strewn with brightly colored pillows that was set at one end of the room below two latticed windows. For the first time since crossing the Golden Horn, David felt the cool breeze and took a deep breath to calm himself.

"Now," said the pasha, "you may lower the hood, but only in here. I have no desire for anyone in the palace, save for the sultan and me, to see your face."

"My thanks, Your Excellency," David replied, pushing his feelings and anger at the pasha's audacity somewhere deep into his brain for another occasion. "It has been a long journey to get here, but I am eager to hear what you and His Highness require of me."

The pasha clapped his hands and nodded his head. "Excellent. I appreciate a man who wishes to get to the crux of the matter without so much as a thimble-full of sycophantic drivel."

"Focus is the critical element for the work my family has performed over the centuries."

"Yes, yes, and I'm sure the sultan, who has the responsibility of a man but the mind of a boy, will want to hear all about it. But we have only thirty minutes before he summons us, so let me give you the background you will need."

"Before you do that, Your Excellency, may I enquire as to how you got my name?"

"Your services were recommended by two European Jewish leaders who must remain anonymous. They were made aware of you by your old client David Sassoon, who now resides in Bombay."

"Ah," said David. "I have not seen Sassoon Effendi for many years. I am pleased he remembered me."

The pasha held up two hands to stop any reminiscing before it began. "Have you heard of the island of Rodos, or Rhodes as the Europeans call it?"

"Yes, it is one of the *Oniki Adalar* and the largest of the Ottoman islands. I have knowledge of much of the Empire and its citizens."

The pasha let out a snort that dripped with cynicism. "So, you are an educated killer? Well, that will save time."

David stood up and gave the pasha a small bow. "Your Excellency, I am uncertain what you were expecting, but I assure you I possess more than a rudimentary education. To simply label me a killer does a disservice to a profession that has been of service to sultans and princes for countless generations. As I said, it's been a long journey, and I am here at your behest, not because I seek favor or reward."

"You're extremely sensitive for someone with such a gruesome occupation. Nevertheless, your admonition—and I perceive it to be such and take no offence—speaks to your professionalism, which is deserving of respect. So, if you would raise your hood and face away from the door, I will have refreshments brought in. What I am about to ask of you, and the sultan will endorse it, should not be heard on an empty stomach."

He stood up, walked to a cord that hung near the door, and pulled it. David could hear a bell ringing. Seconds later, the door was opened, and the pasha ordered coffee and pastries while David looked out the window across the Bosporus and decided that his initial impression of the pasha may have been made in haste. He clearly knew what he was doing in challenging David, and the fact that David had remained calm and determined under provocation had satisfied whatever concerns the pasha may have had regarding his assignment.

"Now," said Reşid Pasha, popping a small cake into his mouth and licking the honey from his fingers, "let me tell you of a situation that took place in Rhodes in February of this year." His account of the blood libel was short and to the point. Any emotions or sympathies he held for the Jews of Rhodes remained private, and by the end of his tale, David was unclear on just whose side the pasha stood—that of the officials involved in the crime, or that of the victims.

When he'd finished speaking, the pasha looked at David carefully. "Well?" he asked. "How do you feel now that I have laid out the facts?"

"The same as I felt before, Your Excellency."

The pasha looked at him in amazement and shook his head. "What is wrong with you, man? Surely you feel horror at the viciousness of the acts visited upon your brethren. You are a Jew, after all."

"Yes, and as a Jew, I am accustomed to intolerance and inhumanity practiced by those of other races and religions against us, whom you call *dhimmis*[7]."

"Perhaps, but other than the *jizya*, which is a small enough tax, *dhimmis* are treated well by the Ottomans, no?"

"Your Excellency," David said, determined to avoid the barbs that Reşid Pasha threw into every question, "I am not here to complain or even discuss the status and treatment of the Jews. I am almost certain that you have a job for me—"

"Very well," interrupted the pasha. He stared for a moment into his empty coffee cup and then looked up at the blank stare of the man who seemed impervious to provocation. "I apologize if some of my questions and statements came across as taunts, but I have not met someone of your profession before, and I wanted to see if you could remain impassive. The job I am about to send you on will require as much dispassion as you can muster if you are to succeed."

"It is the only way I know, Your Excellency. Those of us who inherit the *sica* are taught never to form an attachment, positive or negative, to individuals we are commissioned to eliminate."

---

[7] *A dhimmi is a non-Muslim who is granted protected status under Islamic law in exchange for paying a tax called jizya and adhering to certain restrictions.*

"Yes, I can see the benefit. So now let me fill you in on what the sultan and I require of you. You have heard of the Tanzimat?"

"I have not."

"It is a long and complicated group of reforms that I myself had no small part in creating." Reşid Pasha flicked his hand as if brushing off a compliment that never materialized. "It calls for the establishment of new institutions to replace the primitive laws of our past. I won't waste your time with the details."

Thank God, thought David, who didn't believe his mind could handle a litany of legal jargon.

"But in essence," the pasha continued, ignoring the blank look on David's face, "it guarantees security for the lives, property, and honor of all citizens and subjects of the Ottoman Empire, regardless of their religion or race."

"So, the new Tanzimat rules were ignored or broken by the governor of Rhodes?"

"Precisely. The man acceded to the demands of the European consuls without even questioning their motives. He is a weak and incompetent fool, and we've taken the necessary steps to remove him from office."

"It is this man you want me to assassinate?"

"No, of course not. It is the consuls that we wish you to get rid of." He looked at the ornate carriage clock on his desk. "Now we must hurry. The sultan will be expecting us."

Chapter 9

D avid, his hood pulled low so that it obscured his face, followed the pasha down a long corridor until they arrived at a set of double wooden doors guarded by two soldiers who stepped aside when they recognized the foreign minister. Reşid Pasha tapped on the door with his flywhisk and then opened it.

"My Padishah," he said as he stuck his head round the doorframe, "I have with me your subject from Baghdad."

"Oh, come in, please. How exciting this is," said the youth, lounging on a chaise covered in gold cloth and getting his toenails filed by an older woman in a pink silk robe wearing a fez dripping with gold chains. "You may go," he said to her. "You can do my other foot later."

The young sultan stood up and slipped his partially pedicured feet into velvet slippers. Then, as soon as the woman had left and the doors were closed, he walked up to David and pulled back his hood.

"Oh," he said, sounding slightly disappointed, "you don't look like an assassin."

"Your Highness," David replied, giving the sultan a low bow, "I am also a carpet seller."

The sultan raised his eyebrows and nodded his head in understanding. "I see . . . yes, that makes sense. An assassin who looks like a carpet seller. How brilliant."

"Thank you, Your Highness," said David, smiling at the young sultan. "Stealth and surprise are key in my line of work."

"My Padishah," interrupted Reşid Pasha, "I have filled the assassin—"

"You mean the carpet seller," corrected the sultan, tapping his nose in what he thought was a conspiratorial gesture.

"Yes, I mean the carpet seller," the pasha said with just a hint of exasperation creeping into his voice. "I have filled him in on the situation in Rhodes and, without yet disclosing names, told him that it is the European consuls whom we wish him to eliminate."

"Excellent," said the sultan, lying back down on the chaise and indicating two chairs for David and Reşid Pasha to use. "Now you can tell me all about yourself and this mysterious *sica* that our French and British visitors mentioned when we met with them."

"The *sica*, Highness," David said, "and those who use it, have out of necessity been cloaked in secrecy for nearly two thousand years. We are sworn to protect our heritage on pain of death, and a dead assassin would be of no use to you. All I can say is that ours is a family business that can trace its lineage back to the Roman occupation of Judea."

"Well, that's not very satisfactory," scowled the sultan. "You know, if I wanted to, I could have you tortured until you told me everything." His face contorted in what David could only imagine was a royal pout, and he turned his back on his visitor.

"Oh, my Padishah," Reşid Pasha said, standing up and walking over to where the brooding boy lay. "You are the genius who has just enacted the Tanzimat. Think how your enemies would rub their filthy hands in glee if you were the one to disregard them. Come, come, Padishah, you are a great sultan. You must always come across as such. It is only fair that our assassin retains his anonymity."

The sultan turned around and stared at David. "Oh, very well. Then so be it, but I need something to call you other than 'carpet seller' or 'assassin.'"

"Why not call me 'The Golem,' Highness?"

"Golem? What on earth is a 'golem?'"

"A golem is a mythical creature created from mud that, when brought to life by a rabbi, protects the Jews from their oppressors. There's more to it than that, but that is how I understand the legend."

"You're saying you're a golem?" asked the sultan, sitting up.

"Not literally, but for the purposes of this assignment, that is what I will be."

"Yes," said the sultan, nodding his head vigorously. "I like it. Don't you like it, Mustafa?"

"Indeed, I do, Padishah. He will be 'The Golem of Rhodes,' exacting revenge on those who dared to exert their arrogant Western influence on Yusuf Pasha, inducing him to commit unspeakable crimes and then vanishing back into the mist."

"I think you mean the mud," corrected the sultan.

"Thank you for rectifying my slip, Padishah."

"Then," said Abdülmecid, the teenage ruler of the vast Ottoman Empire, "you will hasten to Rhodes and carry out our orders. Do stop on the way back to Baghdad. I will want a full account of your adventures. But only if you're successful, of course."

David stood up and bowed. The sultan gave him what appeared to be a friendly wave and then picked up a piece of paper and began to read its contents.

"Thank you, my Padishah," Reşid Pasha said as he and David retreated to the door. "I shall keep you informed of our progress."

"Before we discuss payment or expenses," said the pasha when they were once again seated in his office, "this is a list of the people you must dispose of." He handed David a small piece of paper that contained five names: F.G. Wilkinson, British vice-consul; von Sturmer, Austrian vice-consul; von Königsmark, Prussian vice-consul; A. Rottier, French vice-consul; Massi, Swedish vice-consul. David looked at it for a moment and then handed it back.

"What's the problem?" asked the pasha, looking puzzled.

"Nothing," David replied. "I have memorized them. It doesn't pay to have evidence in one's possession."

The pasha gave an approving nod. "Hmm, well, in that case, do you have any questions?" he asked.

"Many," David replied. "While I know where Rhodes is and of the corrupt ways of those in charge, I am unfamiliar with the nature of the place."

"What do you mean?" Reşid Pasha asked.

"I mean, is it a place that welcomes visitors? Will I be singled out as someone to watch? If I am to masquerade as a tradesman, then what sort of trade is conducted on the island?"

"That's a lot of questions for a master assassin. I would have imagined you'd work some of those out for yourself."

"A master assassin I may be, but I am alive because I take no chances in preparing for an assignment. My normal commissions involve one target, but you have given me five. I cannot simply slip in and out."

"I see your point," the pasha said, stroking his moustache thoughtfully. "Allow me to think on this over the next day. I will send a message to you at your residence by this time tomorrow. The person I send will be the eunuch who brought you here today. He is someone you can trust."

"Does he know the details of my commission?"

"No, that is something known only to the sultan and me at this stage."

"And, Your Excellency, in my opinion, that is how it must remain."

"I will make that decision. However, you may rest assured that the eunuch does not know why you have been hired, only that yours is a vital task given to you by the highest personage in the Empire. Of course, eunuchs are as crafty and cunning as baboons, so who can say what he really knows? So be careful of what you say to him."

"Very well, and at the same time, we can discuss my fees and expenses."

The pasha shook his head. "You Jews always come back to the money, don't you?"

"At least we ask politely for what is ours rather than storming in and taking it from some reluctant soul." There was a smile on David's face, which threw the pasha for a second. Then Reşid Pasha laughed.

"My dear Golem, as I shall now call you, I like you. You parry my verbal assaults with good grace and ease. That fills me with confidence as to your abilities. I believe you will find the sultan most generous in this matter. All of that will be revealed tomorrow morning when you meet with my eunuch. Now, I will show you to the staircase entrance. You go down two floors—"

"I remember the way, Excellency." David tapped his head.

"Of course you do. Then I will wish you goodbye and good luck, for I will not see you again. Forget what the sultan said about returning to report on your successes and instead return to Baghdad on completion of your task. I will know your progress. May whichever God you worship go with you."

"Thank you, Excellency, but I prefer to travel alone."

The pasha grinned and gave David a wave as he entered the staircase.

On the way back, David wondered about the pasha's statement that he'd know of David's progress. It could only mean one thing: he'd have spies watching David. That went against every principle and instinct he had. The more he thought about it, the more uncomfortable he felt, though what he could do about it without incurring the wrath of both the pasha and the sultan, he didn't know.

Chapter 10

The next morning, seated at the same table at a discreet distance from the European guests, David was once again told by the hotelier that he had been summoned to a coach parked in front of the reception area.

"*Merhaba*," said Amrani Lahlou, using the less formal Turkish greeting. His greeting, however, was the only thing about the eunuch that was less official that morning. He was dressed similarly to how he'd been dressed the day before. His face was solemn and his expression pained as if he'd just swallowed something disagreeable.

"Do hurry up and get in. We will drive to one of my many houses where we can speak freely. It is not far, and there is no need for you to wear the hood."

"Thank you," said David, who'd forgotten the hooded robe at the hotel. "I look forward to hearing the pasha's plans."

"As I'm sure you do your fees for the task." The eunuch gave a derisive snort.

"Why do you all bring that up as if it were some unsavory piece of marketplace gossip?"

"It is a well-known fact that Jews are obsessed with money."

"Is it? Are Jews more focused on money than other races?"

"Yes. You don't hear Turks talking about it."

"And yet the first piece of information you gave me this morning was that you have more than one house. It's my observation that those who don't have money are, by force of circumstances, focused on how to acquire it, and those who possess a fortune are focused on how to keep it, add to it, and let everyone know they have it."

"You are wrong. We see money as a necessary evil, while to you it is a filthy obsession."

"Once again, your thinking is limited and your words arrogant in this regard. Do you judge an entire people by rumors and the words of bigoted men?"

"How dare you criticize me? I am the chief advisor to a man who is second only to the sultan. I could have you bastinadoed."

"My dear Amrani. It is not a good idea to threaten me. I doubt if the sultan—or the pasha, for that matter—would approve."

For a second, the eunuch's face seemed to collapse into his multitude of chins in a gesture David mistook for fear. "But there is no need for ill-feeling and threats," he continued in a more placatory tone. "Allow me to explain what I meant. Money itself is not the objective of anyone's desire. Not Jew, not Muslim, not Christian. It is what it can acquire for the possessor that matters to all of us. Acquisitions allow us to rise from the dregs of the society into which Jews are thrust by those who consider us inferior. It may be, as the Christians tell us, hard for a rich man to enter the Kingdom of Heaven, but it is impossible for a poor man to enter the palace of a sultan."

The eunuch looked at him thoughtfully for a moment and then gave him a dismissive wave, and David knew that there was nothing he could say that would cause Lahlou to think differently. It was times like these when he wondered whether he'd be doing the world a favor by eliminating the eunuch. But he owed the world no favors, and his father had told him that the *sica* was not to be used for personal vendettas, and so he sat back and looked out at the houses as they passed. A few minutes later, the coach pulled through a large iron gate and up a short stone drive to a white marble mansion that glimmered in the mid-morning sunlight.

The wooden door, covered in latticed woodwork and brass, was opened by a servant in a long white robe who bowed deeply to the eunuch, though not to David.

"This way," the eunuch said, pointing to another set of doors that led onto a balcony with a grand view of the Bosporus. Two divans strewn with bright silk pillows had been set up under a white awning, and a large bowl of figs and dates stood on a table between the divans.

Lahlou ordered the servant to bring tea, plopped his corpulent frame onto one of the divans, and indicated David should sit on the other.

"Now," he said, "let us get down to business, for there is much to discuss before the ship you are to take to the Island of Rhodes leaves tonight on the late tide." He looked at David carefully to see if he'd react to the short timeframe, but David, who was more concerned with the details than the timing, remained impassive.

"Has the pasha decided on a suitable guise for me?"

"The pasha has decreed that you should take on the role of an emissary of the Sublime Porte. Your title is *Reis ül-küttab*, a title that, until the beginning of the Tanzimat, was the position just below foreign minister. It carries with it enough rank for you to be treated with dignity most likely far in excess of what you are used to." He said the last part under his breath as if saying it to himself rather than his guest, who was doing his best to keep his temper under control.

Lahlou continued, "As I understand it, you are being sent to Rhodes to ensure that the Tanzimat reforms are being implemented on the island and to report on any transgressions. The nature of this position will afford you access to the European consuls and ensure that you are treated with the necessary respect by the local officials. In essence, you will be a person above suspicion. I assume you speak more than Arabic?"

"I speak a number of languages, including English and French, though perhaps not as fluently as the pasha, who I am told speaks both English and French as if he'd been born in those countries. In addition, I speak very limited Greek."

"Good, then you will be able to speak to the consuls without a translator. Your inability to speak Greek is of no consequence as your clerk and servant both speak it."

"What?" asked David, failing to keep the anger out of his voice. "No one said I would be accompanied by a retinue. I work alone."

The eunuch tented his fingers. "Both are trusted implicitly by the pasha. They know you work for him, but they have been told that your true identity is to remain a secret on pain of death. They do not, however, know the real purpose of your mission. Neither do I, but I assure you it would be in your interest to inform me. That way, I can ensure your safety."

"On the contrary, maintaining your ignorance is the only way I can ensure your safety—and the safety of the clerk and servant. It doesn't matter whether they have been promised death; if they are caught by the wrong people, they will be tortured, and no one can withstand torture."

"The new Tanzimat reforms specifically ban torture in interrogation," said Lahlou. "However, even if they didn't, the same principle would apply to you, would it not?"

"Certainly, but without the other two, the probability of my being caught is reduced by two-thirds."

"Do not try to beguile me with mathematics. The simple fact is that they are going with you. That is the pasha's demand, and so it must be."

"Then I must refuse the commission." David stood up and made to leave without a clue of how he'd get anywhere, let alone home.

"I would not leave if I were you. Your family is in Baghdad." He paused, leaving the threat hanging in the warm morning air.

David went cold. "My family? You dare to bring my family into this . . . this ill-fated scheme?"

"At the moment, they are perfectly safe," said the eunuch, "and Reşid Pasha desires it to remain that way."

David took a deep breath and closed his eyes to calm himself before he threw his father's admonition that the *sica* was not for personal use aside and killed the toad-like creature that lay on the other divan.

Then the eunuch gave a low cackle. "Come, come, Smulian-Hasson Effendi. As you remarked earlier, there is no need for ill feelings and menacing warnings. No one wants the outcome of your mission to be compromised, just as no one wishes any harm to come to your family. The fee, five hundred Venetian gold ducats, will surely make you an extremely wealthy man for a long time."

David knew he was trapped. While the cavalier way he'd been assigned a retinue made him angry, the implied threat to his family left him cold and furious.

"So be it," he said, sitting back down again. "It appears I am committed whether I like it or not. But you should understand that if harm should befall my family, then I assure you—"

"Be very careful before you threaten a servant of the Sublime Porte."

David gave a thin smile and nodded his head as if he understood. "The fee, by the way, is generous, but I shall earn every *kurus*. I assume, though, it does not include expenses for travel?"

"No," replied the eunuch with a sneer. "I expected you would ask that. Your clerk will cover all expenses, and between him and your servant, they will take care of all your needs. The gold ducats will be in a chest that your clerk will keep safe for you. Now, let me tell you the details."

Over the next hour, he explained to David the responsibilities of the *Reis ül-küttab* and laid out the current situation in Rhodes.

"New clothes will be delivered to your hotel on your return this afternoon," said the eunuch. "You will have to dress as an official of the Empire, not some lower-class ruffian."

"I'm glad your master—and the sultan, for that matter—think more highly of me than you do." David laughed. "While I don't believe I resemble a ruffian, as you so elegantly put it, I knew I'd need different clothes. So, despite your intention, I am in no way insulted."

The eunuch waved off David's interruption. "A message has been sent ahead to the new governor to expect you," he continued. "He knows you are there as an observer, not an implementor, and so he will stay out of your way. Reşid Pasha suggests that you keep your name, drop the Smulian part, and change Hasson to Hussein and David to Dawud."

"So, in other words, take on a totally different name."

"You are not an easy man to like," said the eunuch, giving an exasperated sigh.

"It is my experience," replied David, "that one only needs to be liked by one's friends and family. Seeing as you are not family and having shown yourself not to be a friend by your threats, I see no reason for you to like me, nor me you. Let us conclude our business, and after I leave, there should be no reason for us ever to see each other again."

"Good luck then, Golem," said the eunuch with a smile. "That is what you wish to be known as, is it not?"

"I don't know what you're talking about," David replied, standing up and walking to the door. He cursed the pasha for mentioning "golem" to the eunuch, but there was nothing to do about it now. In any case, it was obvious that Reşid Pasha had lied when he said the eunuch would not know the real assignment. The whole mission had the stink of a fish market at the end of the day.

David doubted he'd have any use for the golem sobriquet in Rhodes. In that he was wrong. When he did see Amrani Lahlou again, he wondered if perhaps he'd been a little hasty in rejecting him as a friend or for failing to kill him.

Chapter 11

When David returned to his hotel, he was informed by the manager that his new wardrobe had arrived and that a tailor was on standby to make any necessary alterations.

"I have four sets of clothes for you, effendi," said the tailor. "Two uniforms for formal wear and two stamboulines." David looked at the uniforms, which were both of a dark navy blue. One had solid blue frogging and the other gold-trimmed epaulettes. The stamboulines consisted of black frock coats and tight-fitting grey trousers. Two fezzes were provided, as well as ankle-high boots of soft black leather that almost, but not quite, fit.

When he'd tried them on and the tailor had pinned the necessary adjustments, David asked him to make the lower part of the left pant legs looser. He didn't tell the tailor that he needed easy access to the *sica*, and the tailor, accustomed to odd requests from his self-important and arrogant clients, didn't question him.

"I will have them delivered directly to your servant at the dockside by this evening, effendi," the tailor said, gathering up the clothes and retreating respectfully.

At five thirty, a coach arrived to take David to the harbor. Inside was a young man dressed in a loose white jacket and pants. He wore a turban and introduced himself only as Eskender.

"I am to be your clerk for the duration of your stay in Rhodes, effendi," he said.

"I am pleased to meet you, Eskender," David said, nodding his head. "I am told you speak Greek, though you do not look Greek."

"No, I am from Ethiopia. I was sold to a Greek merchant when I was only five years old and then to Reşid Pasha when I was fifteen. In his household, I became a scribe and then a clerk. He has tasked me with making sure you are successful in your undertaking."

"And do you know what that is?" David asked, watching the young Ethiopian closely to see if he knew his secret.

"The pasha did not make me aware of that, effendi. All I know is that your mission is of vital importance to the sultan. I am to help you navigate through the various situations you may encounter and provide guidance when you deem it necessary. That is all I have been told. I know nothing more."

"Thank you for being truthful," David said, looking solemn. He'd watched Eskender carefully, looking for signs of untruth—flaring nostrils, darting eyes, twitching fingers—but saw none. If Eskender was a liar, he was a skilled one. "I will rely on you to help me with the officials and directorate in Rhodes."

Eskender nodded. "I shall have my eyes open when needed and closed when not."

"Then you and I will get on perfectly. You have my gold?"

The clerk patted a wooden and iron box on the seat next to him and handed David a key. "There is another chest that contains the money for our expenses. Sha Hakuz, who waits for us at the harbor, has it."

David was expecting Sha Hakuz to be a mature matron of middle age. In this, he was wrong. The woman who waited patiently beside three cedarwood chests was anything but old and frumpy. Sha Hakuz was tall and slim with long hair the color of wheat, which she wore under a diaphanous silk scarf. She bowed her head when she saw Eskender and David and then looked at him with the first blue eyes he'd ever seen.

"Good evening, effendi," she said in a voice that was respectful but showed not an iota of intimidation. "I have all your clothes as delivered by your tailor not an hour ago. I have also purchased other items necessary for a comfortable trip aboard the *Eser-l Hayir*." She pointed at a large paddle steamer belching smoke that danced like a dervish in the evening breeze.

David did his best to appear indifferent, but the thought of traveling on a ship that was not powered by the wind or oarsmen thrilled him, and he had a hard time hiding his excitement.

"You have been on many steamships, effendi?" asked Eskender. For a moment, David thought of lying and saying he had (though not one that small), but he knew Eskender and Sha already knew he wasn't what he purported to be, and so he decided to be as honest with them as he could.

"No, Eskender, I've never been on a steamship, and so I look forward to this experience. What about you? Have you been aboard one of these smoke-spewing behemoths?"

"I have, effendi, when I accompanied Reşid Pasha to the city of London."

"London," said David, looking at his clerk in amazement. "You've been to that fabled city? Is it as magnificent as I have heard?"

"In certain ways it was, effendi, but as a slave, I was not permitted to venture out. But I see that Sha has given instructions to the porters on where to stow the bags, and so I believe we should board the ship."

At the top of the gangway, they were met by a steward dressed in billowing white pants and a snug-fitting jacket with brass buttons who showed them to a small stateroom. Here, Sha began to unpack one of the chests containing David's clothes and stowed them in the closet.

"This room seems tight for three people," David said, eyeing the small divan and two lounge chairs.

"This is yours, effendi," Eskender said. "Our quarters are in a different part of the ship. We will check on you each day, but we are not permitted to mingle other than to carry out our duties while at sea."

"What nonsense is this?" cried David. "I will inform the captain or whoever is in charge that I want you with me at all times."

"That cannot be, effendi," said Sha with downcast eyes. "We are slaves, and we must do what is required."

"I don't understand," David said. "Surely if Reşid Pasha entrusts you with my well-being and permits you to travel out of the capital, you are not slaves in the sense that I perceive the word."

"Reşid Pasha entrusts us with much, effendi. We are part of his household and treated as such," Eskender said patiently.

Sha smiled. "But we are still slaves."

David shook his head. He was both saddened and bewildered. The very idea of slavery was distressing, but the idea of people with the freedom to do anything but be free confused him. He was determined to find out more about his newly acquired possessions, though he realized that it would be a distraction from the assignment he'd been given. In David's profession, distractions were the ultimate sin.

He wondered about the relationship between Eskender and Sha. They were both young and extremely handsome, both at the peak of their sexuality. And yet he sensed neither tension nor lust. It was worrying. It shouldn't have been, but he'd had no choice in the matter of their service, and he couldn't afford any turmoil. He decided to push his concern aside for the moment.

David had just settled into his cabin and was wondering what the protocol was for dining when the same steward who'd shown him to his cabin knocked on the door.

"Captain Sancar has invited you to join him and the other passengers at his table for dinner this evening, effendi."

"Please offer my thanks to the captain," replied David. "I shall be delighted to join him. May I enquire as to time and dress?"

The steward gave a small bow. "Naturally, effendi, with distinguished passengers such as yourself and others, the dress is always formal. Dinner will be served in an hour from now, and I shall return to escort you. May I ask your manservant to help you dress?"

"You may indeed," replied David, who realized his knowledge of decorum was sadly lacking. He hoped that Eskender could provide the guidance he'd need to survive the dinner.

David met Eskender on the deck nearest his cabin, where they stood for a few minutes watching the great capital of the Ottoman Empire vanish into the night as the ship chugged slowly, its massive paddle wheels slapping the water, through the Sea of Marmara toward Rhodes.

Chapter 12

"**I** have been able to ascertain the identities of your fellow passengers, effendi," said Eskender, looking around to see if anyone else was in earshot.

"That is excellent," David replied. "I was wondering who they'd be. Is there anyone I should be wary of?"

"That is hard to say, effendi. There are only three others, and they are of different backgrounds and even nationalities."

"Enlighten me."

"There is a wealthy wine merchant on his way home from Constantinople to Çanakkale, which I believe we will reach sometime tomorrow. His servant says that his only interest is the problem caused by the drought on his vineyards and the tax on his wine."

"I know very little of either."

"There is no reason that you should, effendi. The *Reis ül-küttab* has more important issues to deal with. The second passenger is a woman from England. She is an author, of all things, and has been traveling extensively in Italy and Germany of late but took a short diversion to see Constantinople. You and one other passenger are the only ones on board who speak English, so you will no doubt be able to speak to her. I am told she enjoys fame in her country."

"My English is passable, but I am by no means fluent," said David.

"Then you will be in the same position as the last of the passengers. He is from the country of Prussia, a nobleman by the name of Count von Konigsmark. I believe he was just in Baghdad."

As carefully as David tried to control his surprise, he could not conceal it from Eskender, whose very existence was predicated on his ability to recognize and anticipate changes in the mood of his masters. A raised eyebrow, a lower lip curled at the corners, a clenched fist. Some subtle, some not. Eskender had learned that all were indications of unpleasantness to come.

"Do you know this man, effendi?" he asked respectfully.

David hesitated for a moment, trying to decide how to respond. Then he looked Eskender in the eye and concluded that the Ethiopian already knew the answer.

"No, I don't know him, but I know of him if this count is indeed the same man I am thinking about. Do you happen to know if he was a consul for Prussia on Rhodes?"

"I believe that to be the case, effendi, though I don't know whether he still holds that position. I can enquire of his servant if that is your wish."

"No," said David, his mind beginning to whirr at the possibilities of providence placing one of his targets within stabbing distance so early on in the assignment.

"There's no need to ask any further questions. Although I do wonder what he was doing in Baghdad. You told me earlier, Eskender, that you would have your eyes open when needed or closed when necessary. I may ask you to close them soon. Will that be acceptable?"

Eskender lowered his head. "As I told you in the coach this afternoon, effendi, the pasha tasked me with ensuring your success. He did not inform me what that success would be, and it was not my place to ask. What I did understand, and in this he was as clear as Afghan crystal, was that the task you had been given was sanctified by the sultan himself. Is that enough to be acceptable, effendi?"

David nodded. He studied the man in front of him and decided that Eskender could be trusted. It was a decision he came to quickly, but not lightly, and it wasn't Eskender's words that gave David confidence but rather the way he'd spoken them. Intelligence and dignity surrounded Eskender like some ethereal aura, and there was no indication that behind it lay duplicity or betrayal.

"Very well," he said, "then I must ask your help in dressing for the dinner as I am unaware of the customs aboard a steamship."

Half an hour later, just as the steward knocked on the door to his cabin, Eskender fastened the last of the frogging on David's uniform. He stood back and looked at his charge.

"Very impressive, effendi. You look, if I am not being presumptuous, like a general born to command."

"I feel more like a tightly swaddled infant," said David, wondering how he'd even reach for his *sica* should the opportunity to take out the count present itself that evening. Not that he thought he'd get the chance so early on in the assignment, but experience had taught him to take advantage of an opening when providence provided it. He'd strapped the *sica* to his left ankle just before pulling on the trousers, and while Eskender had eyed it curiously, he'd said nothing.

The captain's dining room was at the front of the ship, forward of the tall funnel that belched a noxious black cloud that, fortunately for those aboard, vanished in the stiff breeze before it had time to settle over the ship.

"Welcome aboard our humble ferry, *Reis ül-küttab*," said Captain Sancar, giving David a polite bow.

"My thanks, Captain Sancar," replied David, looking around the elegant wood-paneled dining room, which was only slightly larger than his cabin, "but this magnificent ship is hardly a ferry, no?"

"It may be larger and faster than the normal ferries that plow these waters, but a ferry nonetheless is what it is. Though I thank you for referring to it as 'magnificent'. All captains like to be complimented on their ships. May we offer you a drink while we await the other guests? Perhaps a glass of wine from Izmir? Or would you prefer a refreshing pomegranate drink, which does not contain intoxicants?"

"I would be delighted with a glass of wine, though I should by all rights drink the pomegranate juice. The

Sublime Porte does not look favorably on those officials who drink alcohol."

The captain laughed. "We are at sea, where the captain's word is law, and I officially declare that at sea, wine is acceptable to we of the faith. Ah, and here I believe is one of our other passengers."

Mehmet Onay—the wine merchant, an elderly man whose girth made the dining room seem even smaller—was arrogant and cantankerous from the moment he walked in. He barely acknowledged David or the captain and waddled over to where the wine was displayed. His grouchiness increased when he saw that the wine being served by the steward hailed from Izmir and not Çanakkale, where he had his vineyards. When the captain introduced David as the newly appointed *Reis ül-küttab*, his attitude changed, and he informed David that he wanted to discuss some pressing issues related to his business before the ship docked at Çanakkale the following day.

Before David had a chance to reply, they were interrupted by the arrival of von Konigsmark. He had the bearing of someone who'd once been a soldier but whose over-indulgence in the food and beverages of Zur Letzten Instanz restaurant in Berlin had left his saber-scarred face bloated like a pig's bladder. His Turkish was poor, and as no one else spoke German, he was forced to resort to English, with which he was slightly more familiar. Neither the captain nor the wine merchant had more than a few words of English, and so the count made conversation with David.

"I am told, Count, that you were recently in Baghdad."

"Ja, disgusting city. I got out as quickly as I could."

"What a pity," David said. "I lived in Baghdad until the business of the Sublime Porte called me to Constantinople. I always found it quite lovely."

"Lovely! Ugh. If you wanted to see lovely, you would come to Berlin."

"May I enquire as to your business in Baghdad?" David asked.

"I came to engage a man who wasn't even there. A waste of a trip."

They were interrupted by the fourth passenger, an English author who introduced herself as Mary Shelley. David had never met a Western woman before and, at first, was slightly unnerved by Mary's off-the-shoulder dress. He bowed and tried to take in as much of her appearance as he could without staring. Her face was thin and her brown hair pulled back tightly against her head into a bun. Were it not for her eyes—keen and perspicacious behind thin, gold-rimmed glasses—she would have looked like a severe schoolmistress. She nodded to both the captain and the wine merchant and then joined David and the count when she heard them making conversation in English, broken as it was.

"I am told that you're an author of some renown," David said, sensing her shyness and doing his best to sound friendly.

"You are most kind, sir," she replied in a soft voice that did nothing to dispel the sense of intrigue that David felt. "I have had success with my novel, *Frankenstein; or, The Modern Prometheus.* Other books of mine have been treated with no more than a modicum of favor."

"Ugh, woman authors," said Count von Konigsmark, giving Mary Shelley a dismissive sneer. "In Prussia, women know their place, and you won't find them clutching a trivial manuscript to their bosom."

"Indeed, sir," replied Mary, raising her eyebrows. "I believe you to be in error."

"What?" said the count with an even more intense sneer. "You don't believe women know their place in the Prussian Kingdom?"

"I cannot comment on the prejudice with which women are perceived in your country, Count, and I shudder to think how they are treated in your own household, but in my recent travels through other parts of Germany, I met many strong and determined women and read books by several of your female authors. You have no doubt been too preoccupied with affairs of a different nature to have read Adele Schopenhauer, sister of your famous philosopher Arthur Schopenhauer? Or perhaps Bettina von Arnim? She is close friends with Goethe and Beethoven . . . you've heard of them, have you not? Or again, sir, have you been too focused on less intellectual pursuits than poetry and music?"

For a moment, David thought the count would slap Mary. His face went from a light crimson to the color of a ripe pomegranate, and he clenched his jaw till it seemed as if his teeth would crack. Then he took a deep breath, inclined his head, and clicked his heels. He would have stormed off if there had been anywhere to storm off to. He moved over to where Captain Sancar was doing his best to assure the wine merchant that he would speak to the owners of the vessel about changing wine suppliers. This left David alone with Mary.

"And how shall I address you, sir?" Mary asked. "Your uniform indicates a gentleman of some importance."

"I have a formal title," replied David. "It is *Reis ül-küttab,* but I would not dream of using it in the company of such formidable assertiveness. My name is Dawud Hussein. Please, unless it is uncomfortable for you, call me Dawud."

"It is not uncomfortable, but it would be presumptuous. So, I shall call you Mr. Hussein."

David nodded. Clearly, there were rules of etiquette in Western culture that Eskender would need to explain.

"Now, tell me, Mr. Hussein, how it is that you speak English with such uncommon ease?"

"You flatter me, madam. My English is no more than adequate. But to answer your question, I learned it back in my hometown of Baghdad, where my family were, and still are, carpet merchants. We had many buyers from England, and I was fortunate to pick up the language while I was young and then improve it over the years in the court of our sultan—well, not the present one, who is still very young—but his father." David had long ago concluded that a mixture of truth and lies worked far better than all of one and none of the other.

"Baghdad, you say? One forgets how vast the Ottoman Empire is and how enlightened your sultan must be to employ men from all corners of the empire."

"Indeed, but I am most interested in this book of yours . . . *Prometheus*—"

"*Frankenstein; or, The Modern Prometheus* is the title."

"I am familiar with the story of Prometheus," said David, "but I have no idea as to what Frankenstein refers. If it is not an imposition, perhaps you can explain how the two names are connected."

"I should be pleased to tell you, but I see the steward is indicating that we should take our seats for dinner. If I can, I will answer your question at dinner, or perhaps afterwards we can take a stroll on the deck before retiring."

Dinner turned out to be less amicable than the captain had envisaged when he'd seen the list of first-class passengers. Von Königsmark sat scowling at one end of the table, unable to communicate with the captain or wine merchant and unwilling to talk to David or Mary. Mary, who spoke passable Greek, was soon in a light-hearted conversation with Captain Sancar, while the wine merchant harangued David on the lack of respect Ottoman officials displayed for their subjects. David listened politely without hearing a word and promised he'd take it up with Reşid Pasha himself on his return, which seemed to satisfy the disgruntled merchant.

The dinner party, though it was hardly a party judging by the lack of gaiety, ended early with the captain saying he needed to go back on duty and the wine merchant drunk on too much of his competitor's wine. The count left without wishing anyone a good night, and David and Mary walked out onto the deck together.

"Let us go to the front of the ship," Mary said, "away from the sound of the large paddles that slap at the water like angry leviathans."

David clapped his hands. "Ha, an image that could only be conjured up by a formidable writer."

Mary gave him a coy smile. "I'm afraid it was just a cliché and one not worthy of even a bad author."

It was a moonless night with just a light breeze, and as he stared out across the water, David could just make out the island of Marmara on one side and the coast of Thrace on the other.

"Other than the noise of the paddle wheels," he said to Mary, who had removed her glasses as she too stared into the night, "is it not peaceful?"

She nodded in return and looked up, shifting her focus to the stars as if she were remembering something. "It is, though I'd always imagined that the waters that separate two great and differing continents would by necessity of their importance be less than calm."

David laughed. "Perhaps the spirits of the Sea of Marmara believe it is their duty to instill a sense of calmness. But you promised to tell me about your novel and the connection between Frankenstein and Prometheus."

"I wrote it when I was but nineteen years old," she replied. "I was very naïve, but also idealistic and impassioned, and my mind was filled with angst."

"I don't know that word."

"'Angst?' It is a word I picked up in Germany. It means grief or sorrow and a dread of dissatisfaction. And I suppose that may be at the heart of the story, though even after all these years, I find it hard to provide a suitable précis. I'll do my best. The book is about a scientist named Frankenstein, obsessed with creating life from non-living matter, and when he does, he is horrified at what he has created. It is the temptation of man to play God. That is the similarity between Viktor Frankenstein and Prometheus. Both stole from the gods—Prometheus, fire, and Frankenstein, life—and both suffered for their arrogance."

As she told David the story, he began to see parallels with the legend of the golem, and by the time she'd finished, he wondered whether, if she'd known who he really was, she'd see him as the monster or the creator. He did not believe anyone could read the mind of another, but there was something about Mary Shelley's eyes that made him shudder.

"Your face betrays your feelings," Mary said. "Do not be too distressed or judgmental. As I said, I was only nineteen when I wrote it."

"On the contrary," David said. "If I am judgmental, then it is to do with your genius. No, my face betrayed my own thoughts on the subject of mortality."

She laughed. "Ah, well, I have a feeling that is not something you'd discuss with a stranger, but your compliment is well taken and much appreciated. Over the years, I have had to endure much criticism and often been accused of transgressing the rules of both virtue and justice from men who, like that pompous Prussian, believe women to be bereft of imagination."

"And yet you seem unaffected by it."

"I once told my late husband that invention consists not in creating out of a void but rather from chaos, and if that is indeed the case, then one cannot be offended by those who cannot see the chaos that engulfs an imaginary story. For that is all it is. No man—or woman—can create life out of the inanimate. That is the role of God. Do you not agree, Mr. Hussein?"

"I . . . um—"

"You hesitate . . . surely you don't believe that such a thing is possible?"

"No, I doubt that man can create an actual creature as you describe the monster in your book, but I do believe that there are times when God imbues in man the ability to do things other mortals cannot."

"And this is your moral dilemma? Does it center on the creation of life or the destruction?"

David looked at her carefully. He saw the puzzlement in her eyes behind her thick lenses, and he wondered once again if she could read his mind.

The morality of what he did had never confused him. *We cannot exculpate ourselves from the act of killing, so we must focus on the consequences of what the act itself accomplishes,* his father had said when David, at age fifteen, first questioned the long history of an eighteen-hundred-year-old family of assassins of which he was the present incarnation. *It is no different to being a soldier in a battle. The soldier's job is to kill someone who has been designated by his superiors as the enemy. He is not responsible for the morality of his commanders or of his enemy. Only his own. It is the same for us, which is why we must endeavor at all times to be objective. No assassination can be personal.* That was what worried him now, and it was the shadow of doubt that had crossed his face that Mary had seen. He knew the crime of the consuls, and as hard as he might try, he didn't believe his assignment could be objective.

He forced a smile. "Your story has given me much to think about, and it is a welcome distraction from the boredom of administrative work. But it is late, and the wind has cooled the air. You must go inside before you freeze."

She laughed again. "You strike me as a virtuous man, Mr. Hussein, one whose mind is open to the world. I have a feeling you will always do what is right. I bid you a fond evening and look forward to seeing you again before I disembark tomorrow." She touched his arm and disappeared into the ship, leaving David alone on the deck with his thoughts.

Chapter 13

David's thoughts whirled around his head like the sirocco winds that billowed from the desert through the streets of Baghdad, and he was so preoccupied as he strolled up and down the deck that he failed to see the lumbering figure of the count until the man had snatched at his lapel.

"You think, because you are some official of the Ottoman Empire, that you can insult me?" the count said, his words thick and slurred.

David grabbed hold of the count's wrist and easily pulled it from his uniform. "I have no recollection of insulting you, sir. I fear you may have had too much to drink. Please, unhand me, and perhaps go to your cabin and sleep off the wine."

The count spat at David, but the gob was blown off target by the wind. "You filthy Arab," said the count through gritted teeth. "You upstart swine! I will see that you are punished for your insolence towards an important consul for the Kingdom of Prussia. You will lose your position for sure, your life perhaps."

"If I offended you in any way, sir, I apologize."

"You think to make a fool of me with that foul-minded harpy. Why, I should run you through with my Schläger." His words were garbled and his movements awkward. "In fact, that's precisely what I shall do. Wait here while I retrieve it from my cabin, you desert rat."

He turned towards the entrance to the cabins but stopped when David caught his collar.

"Before you go to retrieve what I imagine is your sword, I have something to ask you, a question that comes directly from the sultan himself. If you still feel like running me through after that, I shall be happy to wait." The count paused and David took his elbow.

"This way," he said, leading the inebriated nobleman towards the leeward side, where the paddle wheel creaked and groaned.

"Ask quickly, you son-of-a-sand-whore, for die you shall before the night gets any older."

"Yes, yes," said David quietly, looking around to see if they were alone. "The sultan has tasked me with establishing whether you were one of the consuls in Rhodes during the questioning of the Jew earlier this year?"

"Of course I was. Damn bastard got off too easily. We should have burned him alive for his crime."

"Excellent," David said, bending down as if to scratch his leg and pulling the *sica* from its sheath on his left ankle. "In which case, may I wish you a safe passage . . . to hell." He flipped the confused consul round and drove the blade into his left kidney, drawing it across to sever the right one. Whether the count understood what had happened was unclear. He gave a low moan, hung over the edge of the railing for a moment, and toppled over onto the paddle, which plunged him down into the murky water, lifted him up as it spun around, and then, to David's relief, flung him like a rag doll into the wake.

The stab wound had been so deliberate and almost surgical in its execution that no blood remained behind on the deck, and only a thin film covered the blade of the knife, which the spray from the paddle soon washed off. David slid it back into the sheath and strolled slowly to the door, where he encountered Captain Sancar.

"Did you see the count when you were out on deck?" asked the captain, looking worried.

"No," David replied, feigning surprise. "The last I saw of him was when he left the dinner table and *Hanimefeni* Shelley and I took a stroll around the deck. We were in the front of the ship, so perhaps he walked to the rear when he saw us. Though I doubt he could have walked far; he seemed quite inebriated."

"Indeed, he was," said Captain Sancar. "I hope the damn fool hasn't fallen into the sea. I must find him before he does himself a mischief."

"Here," said David, "I'll come with you."

The wind had picked up, and the ship was rocking from side to side in the heavy swells. "I may have to shut the paddle wheels down," yelled Captain Sancar as he and David scoured the deck looking for the recently departed count. "This sort of weather can damage the paddle shaft."

"Well," he said as they completed their circuit of the deck, "the fool is nowhere on deck. He must have returned to his cabin without his servant hearing him."

"Let us hope so," said David, holding onto the rail as the waves tossed the ship. "This is no place for a drunkard."

"God willing, he is snoring safely in his cabin. It will not look good for me if I have lost a passenger of his importance."

"Fear not, Captain Sancar," David said, putting a reassuring hand on the captain's shoulder. "We all saw that the man was drunk. You cannot hold yourself responsible for the behavior of uncouth dolts."

"And yet as the captain, I am."

"I am *Reis ül-küttab*, and as you decreed with the wine, so do I decree that you are not. Now go back to your duties, Captain, and we will find the count in the morning."

Of course, they didn't, because at that moment, three scalloped hammerhead sharks were busily feasting on the body of the late consul from Prussia.

Chapter 14

David was already awake when Sha and Eskender knocked on the door to his cabin. He'd slept well despite his concern for Captain Sancar, who'd seemed genuinely distressed by the count's disappearance.

"We will be docking in Çanakkale soon, effendi," said Eskender. "It is to be a short stop to allow the wine merchant and English lady to disembark and for the ship to take on more coal. I am informed that the captain will file a report with the local authorities on the unfortunate accident that is believed to have befallen the Prussian nobleman last night. You are aware of what has transpired?" Eskender asked the question so matter-of-factly that David didn't at first pick up on the hint of innuendo.

"Not of its outcome. I helped Captain Sancar search for him on deck. The ship was tossing in the waves, and the captain seemed to believe that he might have toppled overboard."

"The opinion of the crew is that he did indeed fall into the sea."

"That is unfortunate, but Allah has decreed all things through eternity as the Koran teaches us. It was the Prussian's time to die."

David wasn't sure whether that was a legitimate interpretation of the Koran, but it sounded as if it could have been. He hadn't discussed his Jewish "faith" with Reşid Pasha or the eunuch, and he was uncertain what Eskender and Sha had been told about his religious affiliation, if anything. While he had no deep knowledge of the Koran, he knew enough to sound as if he did—certainly to a non-scholar of the holy book.

"Do you believe that fate is already determined, effendi?" asked Sha. "Or do you believe that Allah employs some people as the instruments of fate?"

David went cold. Yesterday Sha had seemed subservient, almost serene in the way she spoke. Now there was an edge to her voice. It wasn't so much what she'd asked, although it was profound for someone in her position, but her tone was more assertive, less assentive. Had she witnessed him on the deck with von Königsmark? He'd looked around and seen no one, but perhaps she'd been concealed by the shadows. In which case, he wondered, who else knew?

"Why do you ask?" He tried to keep the hesitation out of his voice.

"My apologies, effendi. I ask only because I am a recent convert to Islam with a desire to know more of its sacred laws, as all slaves should. Someone of your exalted position is a valuable source of information."

David studied her carefully. As a competent liar himself, he could easily spot the signs of perfidy in others. Or so he believed. None of the familiar ticks and nervous movements were present in Sha's perfectly formed face.

Her eyes were downcast, but he took that more as an expression of deference than fabrication. He looked over at Eskender but could read nothing his face.

"If God wills one to be an instrument in the fate of others, then who are we to question that? But . . . your question is a strange one."

"She meant no offence, effendi," Eskender said quickly, picking up a note of anger in David's voice.

Aha, thought David. *So, he does care for her.* "I did not take it that way," David replied, a little less sternly. "But in my experience, that sort of question does not come from a desire for knowledge. I am not a fool. Now, tell me the truth, and if you attempt to deceive me, I will know it."

Sha raised her head and looked directly at David, any remnant of acquiescence gone. "We are here to take care of your needs and to make sure your mission is successful."

"Oh, really? And who do you work for? Amrani Lahlou, the eunuch?"

"No, effendi," Eskender said. "We work for the pasha, as I told you before we departed."

David took a deep breath and let it out slowly. Things were unravelling. "So, I suppose you know what I was tasked to do?"

"We were told by the pasha that your assignment is delicate but dangerous—"

"—and that we had to ensure your safety and success," repeated Sha, sounding less and less like a slave and more and more like someone experienced in matters of intrigue.

"And so," David said to Eskender, "you lied to me yesterday." He had no idea how he'd missed the clues, but he had, and that concerned him.

"Yes, effendi, and for that I apologize. The pasha was insistent that we reveal only the minimum of what we knew about you until the time came when we could no longer conceal our knowledge. It appears that this is the time."

"So," David said very calmly, though he did not feel it, "you observed me last night on the deck?"

"You were careless," Sha said. "Had we not been there, you would have been interrupted by one of the sailors who was on his way to inspect the paddle wheels."

"Sha detained him until you'd completed your job," Eskender said. "You are most accomplished, faster than anyone I have ever seen."

"Thank you," David said, feeling pleased at the compliment but confused at Eskender's intention. "I appreciate your help, but I was very clear to the pasha and the eunuch that I work alone. By telling you of my assignment, he has put all of us in grave danger."

"Understand, effendi," replied Eskender, "that the pasha always has a reason for what he does and says. If he believed that our knowledge of your assignment would compromise you in any way, he would not have told us. You may rest assured he trusts no one more than he trusts Sha and me. I say that not to appear arrogant—it is merely the truth. We are both experienced agents for Reşid Pasha. You must not doubt our abilities."

David nodded. He could see no way out of the situation, and if what the eunuch had said about the safety of his family was true— and he reluctantly accepted that it was—then there was nothing he could do, at least for the moment. He'd need to think carefully about his next move.

"Now, you must join the others on the deck, and when we dock, Sha will take you to a hammam so that you can bathe. Constant attention to cleanliness is expected of an official."

Chapter 15

As David made his way to the front of the ship to watch its progress into the harbor, he found Mary Shelley standing under a parasol, gazing at the old castle that dominated the city of Çanakkale. She wore a long dress, far too warm for the already climbing temperature, and a bonnet that David thought made her look older than she had the night before.

"This is where I disembark," she said when he greeted her. "So, I must bid you adieu and tell you that I enjoyed our conversation last night. It is always a pleasure to meet someone as much of a listener as he is a talker."

"I shall take that as a compliment," David replied with a smile.

"It's intended that way."

"May I enquire as to why you are visiting Çanakkale?" he asked.

Mary returned his smile. "I have two reasons. The first is that Çanakkale was the finishing point when Lord Byron, a man I once knew, swam across the Hellespont from Sestos, over there." She pointed across the water. "It was

said to be a feat to rival that of the Greek hero Leander."
He noticed her blush as she spoke of Lord Byron and wondered why.

"That is most impressive," David replied, looking
across the Bosphorus towards the Greek mainland at what
appeared to be a pile of rubble.

"Byron was a most impressive man," Mary replied,
sounding melancholier than she had the night before. "He
was a brilliant poet and a hopeless romantic who fought in
the Greek War of Independence. Alas, it was during that
unfortunate conflict that he died."

"To my shame, I don't know of this Lord Byron, but I
sense you were close to him. I am sorry for your loss."

"In England I would have said you presume too much,
but I can tell you are being sincere, and so I thank you for
your sentiments. But there is another reason I am stopping at Çanakkale."

"And may I ask—and please forgive me if this, too, is
presumptuous—what that is?"

Mary laughed. "No, there is nothing in the least au-
dacious in your question. I am most interested in the
mystery of the legendary city of Troy. A friend of my late
husband—the newspaper publisher and amateur geol-
ogist, Charles Maclaren—believes that that hill—" she
pointed to a mound adjacent to the town "—which is
called Hisarlik, is the site of Troy, the famed city that
Homer wrote of in *The Iliad*."

"I have read *The Iliad*," David said, doing his best to
see a city in the shapeless mound, "but I always thought
Troy was more of a fabled city than an actual one. There

is so much about the world that my limited education has failed to reveal."

"What nonsense," Mary said. "You are enlightened, a characteristic which I cannot say exists in many men, and an open mind never closes to the world around us. You seem to me to be a scholar of life who takes in everything you see and hear."

"Well, I am from Baghdad, after all. It was once the greatest city in the world for learning and discovery—alas, no more. But for those of us with a desire for knowledge, the ghosts of the great scholars still walk the streets. Your story of Frankenstein and his creation has given me much to think about."

And indeed, it had. If he was the golem and the golem was the self-destructive monster in Mary's novel, then was he part of a self-fulfilling prophecy? In this troubled and uncharacteristic state of mind, he wished Mary success in her quest and went ashore to look for Sha.

She was waiting for him away from the throng of stevedores and porters. "Please," she said, "follow me. It is not too far." He nodded and walked alongside her till they came to a white-washed stone building with a bronze dome.

Inside the marble and tiled reception area, Sha spoke to the attendant, who argued with her until she handed over some coins.

"Is there an issue?" asked David as the attendant retreated quickly into the interior.

"Not anymore, effendi. I was simply making sure that you have the hammam to yourself for the next hour.

Now . . . ." She handed him a white and blue striped linen peshtamel and a loincloth from a basket to the side of the reception desk just as the attendant returned to assure them that the steam rooms were prepared and empty for the distinguished *Reis ül-küttab* to enjoy his cleansing.

The attendant showed David into a chamber with wooden benches and lattice cabinets, where he assisted him in undressing and then turned away as David put on the loincloth. He draped the big blue and white towel around David's shoulders and escorted him into the first of the hot rooms, which was pleasantly warm and smelled of an unfamiliar, exotic fragrance that made him feel lightheaded.

He sat for a few minutes until he began to sweat, and remembering the routine from his hammam experience at the hotel in Constantinople, he rinsed himself under the cold water that ran from a spout on the glistening, white-tiled walls and went through the arch into the next room. He moved through the increasingly hotter rooms, repeating the ritual until he came to the main room, which contained a large white marble octagonal washing slab under a barrel-vaulted ceiling. The slab was warm to the touch, and he lay on it face down, lulled from his anguished thoughts of the golem into a peaceful reverie that included Sha. He knew it was wrong, that there were too many thoughts intruding into what should have been a highly focused mind, but he couldn't help it.

Then he heard the approaching footsteps of the attendant, who removed the peshtamel, now soaked through with his sweat. He felt a soft sponge begin to lather his body with suds, starting at his shoulders and working its way down towards his feet. When the hands travelled up the inside of his legs and got a little too close for comfort to his scantily wrapped testicles, he opened his eyes. Discomfort gave way to shock and shock to desire when he saw that his sponger was none other than Sha, and Sha was naked.

David jumped up. He opened his mouth to admonish her, but his throat had constricted, and no words came out. Sha put her finger to his lips and patted the warm slab for him to return to position one.

"Say nothing, effendi," Sha whispered. "Just lie down and accept the pleasures that come with your position as an emissary of the Sublime Porte."

"But I'm married," David croaked. "This feels wrong."

"No, effendi. David Smulian-Hasson is married. Dawud Hussein, *Reis ül-küttab* of the most powerful empire on earth, is not."

Whether it was David's already delicate state of mind after his encounter with Mary Shelley or the fact that a woman unlike any he'd met before was applying suds to those parts his wife touched only when he took her hand and placed it there, he found himself falling under the spell of the Circassian slave[8].

---

[8] *Editorial note: I must confess to a great deal of my own angst when I tried to come to terms with David's reaction—the one after he says, "But I'm married." In all of the previous sica stories, none of the assassins— men or women—is married, and they tend to cavort like horny badgers at every opportunity. At the beginning of this story, just before David*

David lay down and closed his eyes. As much as he tried to imagine that it was Ruth running her soapy sponge down his back, unfastening the loincloth, discarding the sponge, straddling him, and completing the ablution with . . .. *Good Lord*, he thought, *could she possibly be using . . . yes, she could.*

When it was over, he opened his eyes and smiled up at Sha. It was a mindless smile that looked to the attendant who'd secreted himself behind a marble column to have portrayed both contentment and confusion. Sha's face, on the other hand, betrayed no emotion. It was as if this were an obligation, an act of duty. There was no acknowledgment of pleasure or gratification. For a moment, David wondered whether, should he ever confess his actions to Ruth, he could say that the other party had remained dispassionate. Sha stood up, took David's hand, and led him to the next room, where cold water ran from a

---

leaves for Constantinople, his wife reminds him playfully "not to covet his neighbor's wife," and it appears, given their petit intimacies and David's thoughts about Ruth while on the road, that their marriage is a loving one. The point is that when Sha tells him to lie down again, he is surprisingly discombobulated and vulnerable. Perhaps it's his reaction to the eunuch's threat to his family or the very poignant message in Mary Shelley's story that causes him to question the ethics of what he does. Certainly, no other bearer of the sica (including yours truly) had any qualms about slicing the odd kidney or liver, and if anything, they saw assassination as their moral duty to rid the world of awful people and degenerates. So, in both of these reactions, David is an anomaly.

marble faucet high up on the wall. When they were clean and cool, they exited the room, and David found himself once more in the dressing chamber where the attendant stood with his freshly washed and dried clothes.

Sha met David in the front of the hammam.

"How do you feel?" she asked as they made their way back to the ship.

"I don't know," he said, because he didn't.

"I believe you will find that your mind has cleared. The hammam has a way of removing the bad humors from the body, returning it to its healthy balance."

"Well, it wasn't just ill humors that my body expelled."

"No, that is a tradition from my tribe, the Abzakh. No warrior goes into battle with full testicles." She then uttered a phrase in a language that David was unfamiliar with.

"What does that mean? What language are you speaking?"

"It is in the Abzahn Adyghe dialect of my homeland. It means 'full balls, full head.'"

"Hmm, very interesting tradition," David said, suddenly realizing that he did indeed feel as if the mist had lifted from his brain. "I know very little of the Circassian homelands. I'd like to know more . . . especially some of the other traditions."

For the first time, he saw what he thought was a smile on Sha's face. "And I shall be more than happy to tell you of my people and our beliefs. But we should wait till we are settled in Rhodes, where we can do so in private. There are too many eyes on a ship."

Chapter 16

"It's said that the great Colossus of Rhodes once stood here at the entrance to Mandraki Harbor," said Captain Sancar as he and David stood at the bow watching as the pilot boat towed the *Eser-i-Hayir* into the harbor. "Now all you have are those two columns with the deer on top staring dumbly out over the sea. What they signify, who can say?" He babbled on about the Castle of St. Nicholaos (which now served as a lighthouse), the medieval city, and the Grand Master's Palace, which stood like some monstrous sentinel overlooking the city.

David heard very little. His mind was now totally focused, as Sha had promised, on the job at hand.

"It was once the headquarters of the Knights of Rhodes," continued the captain, oblivious to the fact that his passenger hadn't heard a word. "Today, it is a palace in name only and I believe used as a prison. The Knights Hospitallers ruled the Island of Rhodes for two hundred years before they were defeated by the Ottomans. It is said they left a vast treasure buried somewhere on the island. Many have searched for it, but to this day it remains undiscovered. Personally, I doubt it ever existed. If legends were true, they'd make for boring stories. Anyway, Rhodes is a beautiful place. I think you will be happy here, *Reis ül-küttab.*"

"What?" David asked, suddenly aware that the captain had been talking to him.

"I said I thought you'd be happy here."

"Happiness is not what I seek. Happiness is what I dispense."

"I don't understand," said the captain.

"There is an old tale from my part of the world in which the great sage, Nasrudin, is asked by a student to tell him where happiness comes from. It comes, said Nasrudin, from making good decisions."

The captain pondered this for a moment before mumbling something unintelligible.

"My job," continued David, "is to ensure that the officials in Rhodes make good decisions in the future, something they have not done in the past. With this, the sultan will be happy, and I will have completed my task."

"And what of these officials?" asked Captain Sancar. "Will they be happy?"

"Let's just say they won't be making bad decisions again." David bit his lip. What had come over him? Ever since his session in the hammam with Sha, he'd felt less daunted. His confidence had returned, and with it a certain hubris. It was something he realized he'd have to control if he didn't want to draw attention to himself.

Captain Sancar nodded his head and grunted his approval. In truth, he had no interest in what his passenger's job entailed. All he had in mind for his short stay on Rhodes was good wine and a visit to a famous brothel located just behind Mandraki harbor.

A gleaming black landau with two bored-looking horses was waiting for David, Eskender, and Sha when they walked down the gangplank. A mustachioed man in white baggy pants and a long blue robe and matching turban bowed to David and then proceeded to talk to Eskender in Greek. When he was done, Eskender translated all he'd said.

"He is an under-secretary to Resit Bey, the temporary governor, who is expecting you at the governor's mansion. I will accompany you there while Sha arranges for our luggage to be transported to the house that the temporary governor has provided for your use while you are in Rhodes."

"Ugh," said David. "So soon."

"Fear not, effendi. My job is to protect you from situations that may cause you unnecessary stress. Remember you are here as an observer, not to pass judgment or give opinions."

"You're right. Well, I have more faith in you than I have in myself in these situations. Let's get on with it." Not for the first time since the governor of Baghdad, Ali Reza Pasha, had sent him to Karbala to remove Za'farani, David wondered what advice his father would have given him about clouding his mind with extraneous distractions and thoughts. He'd probably have reminded him that *we are assassins, not actors. Play the part you were born to play, not the one dictated by your clients.*

He'd loved his father, who'd been a kind and gentle man—other than with his victims, obviously. However, his advice, while well-intentioned, was often incongruous and mostly impractical. At this moment, he had no choice but to roleplay, or he'd never bring this assignment to a satisfactory conclusion.

And so it was with considerable trepidation that the newly appointed *Reis ül-küttab* met with Resit Bey, the temporary governor of Rhodes.

Chapter 17

"My most sincere welcome, *Reis ül-küttab*," said the temporary governor when David was shown into his study. "I hope your stay in Rhodes will be both pleasant and fruitful."

David looked at the portly middle-aged man, trying to decide whether to come across as friendly or intimidating. "Selamün Aleyküm, Resit Bey," David replied, deciding to begin with a more amicable tone. "Thank you for seeing me so promptly and for supplying a dwelling place for my stay."

"It is the very least I can do. You have traveled far to ensure that the new Tanzimat reforms are followed in this troubled outpost of the sultan's empire."

"I am here to observe, not ensure. That, as I understand it, is your job and that of your *kadis*. I am tasked by Reşid Pasha and our new young emperor, Abdülmecid—peace be upon him—to watch as you carry out your duties and to assist you should you encounter any obstacles." David wasn't sure why he'd added the last part, and out of the corner of his eye, he saw Eskender purse his lips.

Resit Bey inclined his head. "My thanks, *Reis ül-küttab*. There are a few issues that stand in my way, as you put it."

"Resit Bey Effendi," Eskander said, walking from the doorway where he'd stood respectfully. "My name is Eskender. I am the assistant to the *Reis ül-küttab* and a member of Reşid Pasha's staff. My master has tasked me with handling the more routine aspects of ensuring that the Tanzimat laws are understood. I worked closely with him when he drew up the reforms."

Resit Bey frowned and stared at Eskender. Then he opened his mouth and slapped his forehead with his palm. "Ah, so you are the famous Eskender, the right hand of Resid Pasha the Great. How very fortunate for us. I would be most appreciative if you could spend time with my judges if the *Reis ül-küttab* permits it."

Eskender turned to David, who shrugged. "Of course, if he feels he can help you ensure the transition, then it will make my job easier too."

Eskender bowed to David, and the governor clapped his pudgy hands in delight. "That is a great relief. As you may be aware, *Reis ül-küttab*, my predecessor left under somewhat of a cloud when he failed to stand up to the European consuls and allowed the terrible treatment of the Jews of Rhodes. No doubt you have heard of some of the tragic events."

"I would not be here if I hadn't, Resit Bey. That very abomination visited upon his subjects is what the Sultan—and Reşid Pasha, for that matter—insists be avoided in the future. I shall meet with the Jewish leaders to determine their security and observe these consuls for any signs of misconduct."

"The consuls are not good men, and they are not necessary in the administration of this island, in my opinion. They only cause trouble. Between you and me, I wish they'd simply disappear, but of course that is not for me to say."

David watched him carefully as he spoke and quickly concluded that the governor was not an honest man. "It is probably not for you to say, though I know—because I was on the same boat as he—that the Prussian consul, von Konigsmark, died quite tragically. So perhaps your wish has been heard."

His attempt at a joke failed, and Resit Bey looked even more perturbed. "I was told it was suicide. No doubt the guilt of his shameful behavior is what drove him to commit such a grave sin."

"Who knows?" said David mischievously. "The others may follow his lead."

After exchanging a few more pleasantries, Eskender and David walked the short distance from the Governor's mansion to the modest, white-washed villa that had been set aside for their stay.

"I hope I was not presumptuous in offering my services to Resit Bey, effendi?"

"As I recall, you did not offer; he asked," replied David. "But in truth, I believe it to be a brilliant idea. You will be on the inside, a good place to be if the governor, whom I sense to be untrustworthy, should consider any recalcitrant behavior."

"That was my thought, effendi."

"And an excellent one it was. So, this is to be our lodgings?"

Sha stood in the doorway of the villa, and David's heart raced. For a moment, he saw Ruth and their children, and then the vision of home vanished, and all he could see was the beautiful Circassian. If a speck of the guilt from his infidelity remained, he pushed it into whatever part of the brain stores those thoughts for later.

David was pleased that both Sha and Eskender had opted for bedrooms inside the villa rather than in the servants' accommodation at the back of the house. They did not join him for lunch, which one of the household servants brought to him as he sat in the *mashrabiya*[9], enjoying the breeze that blew through the latticework of the traditional balcony that faced the Aegean Sea.

He'd just finished a plate of purslane, a dish consisting of stuffed tomatoes and zucchini, washed down with a carafe of strong coffee when Eskender and Sha appeared.

"I have set up a meeting with the leader of the Jews, a Rabbi Israel, who has asked if you could meet with him at the Jewish temple," said Eskender.

Sha gave a dismissive snort. "The presumption of the man."

"Do not judge him harshly, Sha," Eskender said. "After

---

[9] *Terrace feature.*

the torture inflicted on him and the other Jewish leaders at the time of the false trial, he is unable to walk more than a few steps."

If Sha felt the slightest remorse at Eskender's admonition, she did not show it. Her face remained impassive as if she felt no empathy for the rabbi, and that unsettled David—not enough to make her less intriguing but sufficient for him to wonder if someone who'd been a slave her whole life was capable of compassion.

"I am happy to meet him at his place of worship," David said, standing up. "Will you accompany me, Eskender?"

"Yes, I shall go with you to the temple, which is no more than a fifteen-minute walk. But then, with your permission, I must go to the governor's mansion, where I am to meet with a group of his *kadis* to enlighten them on the Tanzimat reforms."

"What about you, Sha?" David asked. "Will you accompany us?"

"No, I need to buy supplies for our stay, but I shall be here on your return. Perhaps then, if your time permits, I shall enlighten you more on the traditions of my homeland."

"I shall make time," David replied, feeling a stirring in his loins and coming to the realization that his musings and misgivings were a waste of energy. He glanced at Eskender to see if his face betrayed judgment but saw none.

Chapter 18

Rabbi Hacham Michael Yaakov Israel lay on a divan in his office at the Kahal Shalom Synagogue. Eskender announced David and then departed for the governor's mansion.

"Forgive me, effendi," the rabbi said to David in Arabic. "I would rise to greet you, but my legs betray me. The doctors say it will be many months until I am able to stand, let alone walk."

"No need for apologies, Rabbi," David replied. "It is I who should be apologizing on behalf of the Sublime Porte after the terrible injustices you've suffered."

"You are most gracious, *Reis ül-küttab,* but is it not, as you Ottomans believe, simply kismet?"

"I'm not sure I understand your question."

"I'm not sure I do either because we Jews do not subscribe to the concept of fate. And lying here thinking of all that has happened over the past months has led me to question my beliefs. Not all, but many. If indeed we are the chosen people, then I fail to see the benefit—unless, of course, the Lord chose us to suffer. But please, sit, and I will have my servant bring us coffee." He reached for a small bell that sat on a table strewn with books beside the divan.

"Why do you think that is, Rabbi?" asked David, who was curious himself as to why Jews believed they were chosen. As far as he had observed, the rabbi was right. Being the "chosen ones" didn't seem to result in anything good.

"I wish I knew. For you, it's easier. All things are pre-destined, and you should not question God's will. That's what your religion tells you, doesn't it?"

"That's as may be," David said, wondering if he should tell the rabbi that he was in fact Jewish and deciding to wait, "but then my people do not think of themselves as chosen."

"Ah, but they could have been," laughed the rabbi. "It is said that God first offered the Torah to the children of Ammon, Moab, Esau, and, of course, your own prophet, Ishmael. And when they all rejected it because of its prohi-bitions against killing and adultery, he went to every other tribe on earth. All rejected it for the very same reasons. The only group left was the Jews, who finally agreed. So, in essence, God didn't choose the Jews; the Jews chose God. So maybe my initial thought about God's responsibility to his chosen people is irrelevant."

"And what is it you believe, Rabbi?"

"Me, I'm a little wary of confessing anything anymore, *Reis ül-küttab.* Last time I did, it was under torture too horrible to think about."

"I understand, but I am not here to question or tor-ment you in any way. The new emperor, together with my superior, Reşid Pasha, and encouraged, 1 am told, by two Jewish leaders, Sir Moses Montefiore and the Frenchman, Crémieux, has issued a *firman*."

"Yes, so 1 am told. It exonerates the Jews of Rhodes, condemns their treatment, and relieves the old governor of his duties."

"Have you had an opportunity to meet the new governor?"

"Not yet, but 1 pray he is of stronger character. The old governor was a weak man, *Reis ül-küttab*." Then the rabbi stopped and held up his hands as if he knew he'd crossed a line. "It is not my place to criticize an official of the Ottoman Empire. Forgive me."

"My dear Rabbi," David said as he leaned in and lowered his voice. "Anything you say to me goes no further than my ears. This, 1 assure you. 1 need you to speak freely. If you doubt my sincerity, then allow me to tell you something which only Reşid Pasha himself knows."

"Be careful," the rabbi said, his voice hesitant. "If 1 were tortured again, I'm not sure 1 could conceal a secret."

"First, 1 guarantee you will not be."

"How can you guarantee this? The vice-consuls are determined to try the Jews again for a crime of which even the past governor's *kadi* said we are not guilty. The Austrian, the Prussian consul, the Swede, and the Englishman, Wilkinson, are powerful men who get what they demand. The worst is Wilkinson's son, who looks for any opportunity to beat up a Jew."

"They will never get what they demand again. They will get what they deserve."

"And what is that, *Reis ül-küttab?*"

"Reckoning. The Prussian has already received his, and the others' lives are in limbo."

"The Prussian vice-consul is dead?"

"It appears he either committed suicide or fell overboard on the voyage here. I was on the ship."

"As I mentioned, *Reis ül-küttab,* we do not believe in predestination in my profession, but the death of this Prussian, well, that feels to me like divine justice. What do you think?"

"In my profession, Rabbi, it is unwise to rely on what you think or what you believe. I work solely on what I know."

"Your profession, *Reis ül-küttab?*"

"*Reis ül-küttab* is no more than a title given to me by Reşid Pasha to facilitate my work."

"So, what is it you do?" The rabbi sounded hesitant.

"Have you heard of the 'golem?'"

"Of course. It is a creature created from clay that, if folklore is to be believed, rescues Jewish communities who are imperiled. But what has a golem to do with anything?"

"You asked me what I do, Rabbi. Think of me as a golem sent here not to rescue you, for others have already done so, but to ensure that you never need rescuing again."

The rabbi stared at David for a moment and then shook his head as if the motion would settle the whirling gears of his brain. "I'm afraid to ask you to explain."

"Then don't. No explanation will satisfy you. My sole purpose in meeting with you is to inform you that certain events may occur here in Rhodes that could directly affect the consuls. I need you and your community to avoid any contact with them over the course of my stay."

"Oh, have no fear of that," said the rabbi, giving David a dismissive wave. "None of us, least of all me, has any desire to come within a mile of those *ben zona*."

David smiled. "Calling the consuls sons of whores to an Ottoman official is probably a punishable offence, but, in this case, I believe you are justified."

"That's twice you have used or understood the language of the Jews. Who are you really, *Reis ül-küttab*?"

"That I cannot tell you. But go in peace, Rabbi, with the knowledge that I am here to right the wrongs."

"Revenge is not something that the Torah encourages, *Reis ül-küttab*. Only God is the arbitrator of absolute justice."

"Believe what you will, Rabbi. I am a rational man, and if God sent the consuls to torture and bear false witness against you, then he sent Sir Moses and Crémieux to rescue you and me to extract justice. I hope that satisfies you."

"It does, at least for the moment. But there are two things you should know, *Reis ül*-küttab, things I have dwelt on as I lie here with only my thoughts to amuse me."

"And what are they, Rabbi?"

"There is a rumor that the boy they say we killed was found alive, though his family have reportedly taken him to another island to conceal the truth. More concerning is that while Istamboli was held in the prison, a group of men concealed in dark robes visited his empty house. For what purpose, I do not know. Istamboli died a few days ago from his treatment, and his house now lies empty. I am certain those men will be back."

"As far as the boy is concerned, I feel we should leave that alone until we can confirm the rumor. As far as I can see, only ill will can come from bringing it up now, while the perpetrators of the crime against you walk around freely. As for Istamboli's house, I shall do my best to investigate who these mysterious men were who entered it and report to you on what I find. Now, I have work to do, so I wish you peace and a quick recovery. I shall see you again."

The rabbi held up his hand as if he wanted David to stay and talk, but before the rabbi could engage him in a further bout of verbal sparring on the dogma he had little time for, David stood up, bowed, and left.

Chapter 19

Edouard Massi, who'd been born in Stockholm to French parents and who represented the Swedish consulate in Smyrna, was back in Rhodes for the first time since the incident that was now being referred to in Europe as a "blood libel." The temporary governor had told him that the Jews, whose torment he'd witnessed (and thoroughly enjoyed), had reportedly been exonerated, were no longer confined to their ghetto, and were now under the protection of the Sublime Porte itself. Massi was furious. This meant the Jews were now free to return to their businesses and would most likely interfere once again with the trade deals he and the other consuls had set up.

Trading had always been a lucrative sideline for the consuls, but most European nations now took a dim view of it, believing that it tarnished the dignity of the office. If their bosses only knew, mused Massi, who and what was behind the whole incident with the missing boy. It had, in fact, been masterminded by the British consul, J.G. Wilkinson, because he believed that a Rhodian Jew named Elias Kalimati, who represented Joel Davis, a

London businessman, was disrupting the consuls' share of the local sponge exports. With Kalimati safely locked in the Jewish quarter, they'd been able to take it back. Now that the Jews were once again free to ply their trade, the conspirators would have to think of another plan.

But it was not only the sponge business that was in jeopardy. Wilkinson had hinted at another scheme that, if successful, would be far more profitable than sponges. In fact, after a night of heavy drinking, he'd promised it would make all of them wealthier than they could imagine.

He'd supplied no details, which made the other consuls suspicious of the Englishman's motives. They'd always believed he looked down on them. Von Königsmark put it down to typical British arrogance, but there was no doubt that Wilkinson used his influence with a mysterious official at the Sublime Porte to gain favor with whoever was in charge of Rhodes. Now he and the new temporary governor were as thick as thieves. As the consuls' suspicions and resentment built, they agreed that they needed to take care of Wilkinson. Von Königsmark had been tasked with hiring a specialist to do the job, but he'd failed to follow through.

"Damn the man," thought Massi, looking at the white Mora clock that sat on his sideboard. "He's half an hour late already. No doubt sweating between the brawny thighs of his Greek mistress, the disgusting swine." He'd invited von Sturmer to join him for dinner to discuss a side deal the Austrian consul and the now-deceased von Königsmark had made with a sponge merchant in Vienna.

"Excuse me, please, sir," said his butler, Charis, a grizzled old soldier from the nearby island of Patmos who'd been wounded in the thigh at the Battle of Navarino during the Greek War of Independence. "The cook says that the food will spoil if it is not eaten soon."

"Tell her it had better not," said Massi, scowling at Charis, "or the two of you—." His unfinished threat was interrupted by the appearance of another servant, who cleared his throat before announcing the arrival of von Sturmer.

The Austrian vice-consul was a fat, balding man with round, gold-wire glasses that did nothing to hide his pig-like eyes. He was sweating profusely in his black frock coat and long grey woolen trousers. Massi, who was at least ten years younger and twenty pounds lighter with thick blond hair and flat blue eyes, nodded to his guest.

"I don't have to tell you that you are thirty minutes late."

"No, you don't," replied the Austrian, taking out a silk handkerchief and wiping his face. "I'm late because I received a note from Wilkinson through his contact at the Porte warning me—all of us—that we are in imminent danger."

"I have no idea what that means—'imminent danger'—what are you talking about, man?"

Von Sturmer sat down on one of the dining room chairs and began to drum with his fingers on the table. He was clearly upset, and he mopped his brow continuously with his now-saturated handkerchief.

"Here," said Massi, pouring him a glass of wine from the carafe on the table. "Take a drink and tell me everything."

"This afternoon, just as I was packing up to leave my office, I received a rather cryptic message from Wilkinson's secretary to say Wilkinson had gotten a warning from his friend at the Sublime Porte."

"The man that Wilkinson refers to as the 'Bollockless Bastard.' And what did the note say?"

"That Reşid Pasha and the young sultan have dispatched a man to Rhodes whose interests may conflict with ours."

"I assume you're referring to the matter of the boy rather than our sponge interests?"

"Am I? The sultan and Resid Pasha couldn't possibly know about what we did. They can't . . . I mean, how could they . . . do you think . . . ?"

"You're blithering like an idiot, man. Pull yourself together and hold steady. No one knows about the boy. It is our sponge exporting business that is in danger, not us. It will be completely finished unless we get rid of the damn Jews."

"But sponges cannot be of any interest to an Ottoman official in Constantinople. No, it must refer to the matter of the boy. Though how Reşid Pasha could know about it is beyond me. There is no question that Wilkinson has betrayed us. And the death of von Königsmark? Well, some say it was suicide or an unfortunate accident. Me? I think it was murder."

Massi held up his hand. "Say no more until I have sent these worthless servants away."

When Charis had cleared what remained of the roast lamb that, despite the cook's concerns, was perfectly prepared, Massi and von Sturmer took their glasses of Koukouzina, a drink distilled from grapes and figs that Massi had acquired a taste for, onto the outside balcony that overlooked the water.

"Speak freely now, but quietly," said Massi. "The wind and water may drown out your words, but the walls have ears."

"What are you talking about, man? Walls do not have ears."

Massi shook his head. "It's an expression. My God, sometimes I despair at your ability to comprehend anything."

"Oh really? Well, I thought it was dangerous to accuse the Jews of murdering the boy. Unlike you, if you remember."

"Perhaps, but you enjoyed the spectacle of his torture like the rest of us. Now, what about von Königsmark? As far as I know, his death was ruled an accident, and there was no reason for him to take his own life."

"Which is why I pose the possibility of murder. He failed to acquire the services of the man in Baghdad—that much we do know. And this official, the *Reis ül-küttab* sent by Reşid Pasha, was on the same boat. According to the captain, very possibly on the deck of the ship at the time the Prussian met his untimely end."

"Surely you don't think he was murdered by an Ottoman official?"

"I'm not sure what to think anymore. I mean, what if the *Reis ül-küttab* knows about the boy? Perhaps he threatened von Königsmark with exposure unless he took his own life, or . . . ."

"You need to take a deep breath, my friend. You are seeing spooks in the dark." Massi noticed the quizzical expression on the Austrian's face. "You are making unfounded assumptions. I'm telling you: this *Reis ül-küttab* is here for reasons unrelated to us."

"I hope you're right. Then the only other explanation is that Wilkinson got wind of our plot to get rid of him and had an agent of his kill the Prussian. But how would he know? As far as Wilkinson is concerned, von Königsmark went to Constantinople. Only you, me, and Rottier knew the reason he went to Baghdad. Do you think Rottier betrayed us? I've always thought he had a rather unsavory relationship with Wilkinson."

"Again, you are allowing your imagination to run wild. There is no possible way that Wilkinson knows anything about our plan for his demise. So, relax. Let's get close to this *Reis ül-küttab*. I am certain he will tell us that he is here for something totally unrelated to anything we're doing."

Von Sturmer mopped his brow with the handkerchief that was by now so wet that it drenched his face every time he wiped his glistening dome. "I suppose you're right. I will try to set up a meeting with the *Reis ül-küttab* and the other consuls. I'm sure between us we can gauge his intentions in Rhodes."

"Very well," Massi said, finishing his drink. "Let's arrange a dinner for him at Wilkinson's place. It's the most impressive, don't you agree?"

Von Sturmer didn't, but he also didn't feel like arguing with the impudent Swede.

THE GOLEM

Chapter 20

The thin white cotton cloth that served as a curtain did nothing to impede the light from the sun as it crept over the bed where David stirred from a night that had been both troubling and satisfying. Troubling because he still hadn't come up with a plan to take out the consuls, and satisfying because Sha had demonstrated another technique the women of the Circassian plains used on their menfolk when their minds were as full as their testicles.

He reached over to where Sha had lain before he fell asleep, but she was gone as she had been the morning before and the one before that. He washed himself from the bowl of lemon water she'd left for him, put on his robe, and wandered into the kitchen area, where he found her preparing a plate of straggisto[10] and figs and the awful dark liquid that served as coffee on the island. Sha looked up and smiled.

"Is your mind as clear as your genitals this morning?"

---

[10] *Strained, thickened yoghurt*

David was still a little shocked at her bluntness, but he smiled back. "I wish. I still have no plan for what comes next, and while it has been no more than a few days, I feel the opportunity slipping away."

She placed the figs and yoghurt in front of him. "It will come. Your mind is stimulated. As one essence drains from the low-hanging receptacles, so another fills the one on top."

David was about to suggest that a further round of releasing might do the trick, but they were interrupted by Eskender, who'd just come from the governor's mansion.

"I have interesting and perhaps even fortuitous news, effendi. The European consuls have invited you to dine with them at the home of the British consul, Mr. F.G. Wilkinson."

"Excellent, that is indeed fortuitous. When is this dinner?"

"It is for tonight, effendi."

"Very well. Go and tell them I'd prefer tomorrow night."

"You have no obligations tonight, effendi."

"No, but I don't want them to get the impression that I am waiting on them. Let them, rather, wait on me."

The consuls were not pleased when Eskender relayed David's message.

"Who does he think he is?" asked Wilkinson, the British vice-consul at whose house the dinner would be held.

"I've already sent my servants to the market to get provisions for tonight. Tell him this is most inconvenient."

"You may tell him yourself, effendi," Eskender replied, doing his best to sound sincere, "when you see him tomorrow night. I am certain he isn't being dismissive, but he is on the sultan's business, and I fear that must take priority."

"You are a cheeky fellow for a slave," said Rottier, the French vice-consul. "In my household, you'd be beaten for the insolent tone I detect in your voice."

"You may suggest that, too, when you see the *Reis ül-küttab* tomorrow evening," Eskender said, making a rapid exit before the consuls could throw any other derogatory words or threats his way.

As he walked back to the villa, he considered his exchange with the consuls. An actual *Reis ül-küttab* would probably take the Frenchman's suggestion, he thought, but he was confident David would simply laugh it off. David was unlike anyone he had come across in the twenty years he'd been a slave, or, for that matter, for the five years before when he'd been a child in Addis Ababa. Both he and Sha knew that David had killed the Prussian consul aboard the *Eser-i-Hayir* on the first night of their trip. He'd certainly not denied it, and while neither Sha nor Eskender knew the precise details of the mission given to David by Reşid Pasha and the sultan, they suspected that the killing was part of it. He knew that the consuls had participated in the trial and torture of the Jews, and he'd been told by a talkative servant that the sponge business was their motivation. But he'd also come to realize that their true motivation was not based on a business opportunity but rather on a deep-seated and ancient hatred of the Jews. This part he failed to understand, as from what he knew of the teachings of Christ, tolerance and compassion were the characteristics of a true Christian.

"You look troubled," David said when Eskender walked onto the balcony where David stood staring out at the city.

"More puzzled than troubled, effendi. Though the things that puzzle me seem to be without an answer and best discussed at another time."

"I can respect that," David said. "But what of the consuls? Will they change their plans for tomorrow?"

"Reluctantly, but yes."

"So, they weren't happy with my demand ... good. That means they'll be even easier to read. Perhaps their uneasiness will help me formulate a plan that at the moment is as elusive as a Tantal."

"A Tantal, effendi?"

"It's the mysterious shape-shifting creature of the Mesopotamian marshes that guards hidden treasures."

"Perhaps Sha and I can help."

"Absolutely not. Look, Eskender, you already know more than I would have wished you to know. That I cannot change, but now it is time for you to close your eyes as we discussed when we first met. Your assistance with protocol and your friendship are all I need."

"And what is it you need from me, effendi?" Sha asked as she entered the room with a basket of fresh fish and vegetables.

"From you, my dear Sha," Eskender said, saving David the embarrassment of hemming and hawing, "the *Reis ül-küttab* needs to experience more of the techniques that made the Circassian horse lords such great warriors."

"Well, the *Reis ül-küttab* will have to wait. Clearly, the methods I have employed thus far have been unsuccessful. Tonight I will show him the 'Splitting of Two Moons,' which comes directly from a book called *The Perfumed Garden of Sensual Delight* and is reserved only for the greatest of warriors."

"You two have no shame," said David, trying to sound stern but failing miserably. "No wonder the pasha does not treat you as slaves. You would be very poor ones indeed."

Whatever the "Splitting of the Two Moons" position was (I could find no reference to it, unfortunately), it had the effect that Sha Hakuz intended because the next afternoon, just before David left to attend the dinner at Wilkinson's house, his plan became clear.

"I need you to do some research," he said to Eskender. "Enquire amongst some of the locals if they have heard of any mythical beasts that haunt the island, especially those who may fit into the category of cryptids. Be discreet, though."

"Of course, effendi." Eskender decided he'd rather not know the reason. "After I have taken you to the consul's house, I will visit the market."

Chapter 21

It took twenty minutes to walk to Wilkinson's house. It was an imposing property with high walls that enclosed a lush garden with lemon, olive, and pomegranate trees surrounding an Ottoman fountain. The house itself was large, much more so than even the governor's mansion, which surprised David as he couldn't imagine a vice-consul in Rhodes being afforded such an impressive dwelling. It was made of the same yellow stone as the Knight's Palace, with large arches and outside staircases leading to the upper floors.

In truth, Wilkinson had bought the place with his own money acquired from the now-troubled sponge business. The house the British government had delegated for their vice-consul was a hovel and far beneath the standards of someone as important as Wilkinson believed himself to be. On Eskender's advice, David wore his official uniform with the blue frogging and a matching fez to the dinner.

"It is important that they see you for who you are, effendi: a high official of the Sublime Porte. I have no doubt they will try to impress you with their knowledge of Rhodes. They will see you as some outside official ignorant of the ways of the world and do their best to belittle you."

"Let them see me that way. I have no desire to impress such evil men. The less they think of me, the better. It will suit my purpose."

"Whatever that purpose may be, effendi."

"Indeed, whatever that purpose may be."

They were met at the dark wooden door to the house by a man who was clearly not Greek or Turkish. He was clean-shaven, and his hair—what little there was of it—was blond with streaks of grey at the temples. The butler (that is what Eskender told David he was called) didn't say a word but indicated that they should follow him. He led them to an inner courtyard even more lush than the outer garden with exotic plants and fountains. A group of men wearing European-style suits was gathered around, smoking cigars and drinking wine.

"My dear *Reis ül-küttab*," said a plump, red-faced man with a balding head and thick, grey mutton-chop whiskers. "Welcome to my humble abode. I am Wilkinson, Her Britannic Majesty Queen Victoria's vice-consul to the Island of Rhodes." His accent, David thought, was very different to that of Mary Shelley's. It was rougher and less refined.

"Peace be upon you," David replied, deciding to use the English form of the Arabic greeting. The consul had not extended his hand in greeting, and so David simply

nodded his head. "How very kind of you to invite me to your magnificent house."

"This little place?" said Wilkinson, looking around as if seeing his house for the first time. "It's adequate for my needs here in Rhodes, though naturally it pales in comparison to my spread in England."

"Really?" David said, trying his best to sound impressed. "Then your English abode must rival a sultan's palace. You are a man who has been blessed by God, Vice-Consul Wilkinson."

"Don't know about that, but I've done alright. Better if that damnable Jew had got what he deserved."

At that moment, the other vice-consuls all moved up to meet David, and the conversation moved into semi-polite questions about the new young sultan and the state of the Ottoman Empire.

"We're being impolite, *Reis ül-küttab,*" said Rottier, the French consul, after a few minutes. "May we pour you a glass of chilled wine? It is Vin Santo from the island of Santorini. Quite good, though not compared to wines from my country."

"Of course," David replied with a smile. "I am well aware of France's famous viticulture. More aware, perhaps, than you of my religion's strict laws against the consumption of intoxicating beverages."

Massi, who'd jostled his way to the front, laughed. "Forgive us, *Reis ül-küttab.* Most, if not all, of the Muslims we deal with imbibe. We just assumed . . .."

"As you will discover, I am not like those of my faith who have allowed Satan to lead them astray. I am on official business of the sultan. Therefore, it is best not to make assumptions on my behalf." In truth, David longed for a glass of the excellent-looking wine, but he sensed an arrogance in the vice-consuls as if they were testing him.

"Forgive us, *Reis ül-küttab,*" Wilkinson said, signaling for a servant to attend them. He ordered a mint tea for David. "We are not ignorant of your customs, only of who you really are. Unfortunately, this is an age of fog and lies, but we have only the desire to get to know and understand you."

"First," David said, feeling the distaste for these men he was doing his best to conceal, "not consuming alcohol is not a custom. It is a law decreed by the Holy Koran. Second, I don't know of this fog and lies you speak of. I am the eyes and ears of Reşid Pasha on this island. I am here to ensure that what transpired but a few months ago does not repeat itself."

"You are, of course, referring to the incident with the Jews who murdered that young boy?"

"I am referring to a miscarriage of justice directed at a group of the sultan's subjects who were forced to submit to treatment that is forbidden under the new Tanzimat reforms." He wasn't sure how accurate he was, but he felt sure his tone and attitude would mask any errors.

"You may not know, *Reis ül-küttab,* that the consuls were mere witnesses to the interrogation of the Jews that was ordered by the previous governor. In fact," said Wilkinson, "we discouraged the torture."

"That is good to hear, sirs. My information is therefore wrong. I must thank you for correcting it. I was told that you were quite insistent upon it."

"Absolute tosh," Wilkinson said, waving his hand. "We are civilized men, sir."

"Are you implying that the Ottomans are uncivilized?"

Wilkinson stammered. "Not at all."

"Well, as you know, the previous governor was dismissed, and the sultan himself issued a *firman* exonerating the Jews. So, from what you're telling me, all the perpetrators of the crime have been punished, and I should declare the affair officially closed?"

"Yes, precisely, *Reis ül-küttab,*" said von Sturmer, the Austrian. "Other than the fact that the Jews have once again stuck their large, greedy noses in our sponge business, all is as it should be. I do not doubt that with your presence, we can once again enjoy a period of prosperity and commerce."

"I am unaware of the issue with the sponges. And to be honest, I don't care. I am not interested in your commercial enterprises."

One of the rules his father had taught him was never to get involved in the affairs of his intended marks. *The more you focus on the reason rather than the act of killing, the less effective you will be,* his father had counselled him.

I'm not sure I understand why?

Very simple. We kill because someone is paying us. We are attached to our mark by money alone. We don't like them or hate them. We don't feel sorry for them, nor do we try to justify their demise because of something bad they've done.

Until this assignment, that's precisely how David had approached his targets. But this job was different. For a start, both Resid Pasha and the young sultan had told him enough about the consuls to remove any detachment. And now, meeting them and listening to the bigotry that spewed out of them like venom from a serpent, it became almost impossible to remain impartial. That said, the less interest he displayed in their gripes and grievances, the more detached he'd appear. He certainly did not want them to believe that he had any interest in them at all.

"Well, we were hoping perhaps you would intervene with the Jews to ensure that they stay out of our business," continued von Sturmer. "We have discussed it amongst ourselves, and we all agreed we would never expect your involvement to go unrewarded."

"Hmm, that makes it interesting."

"Excellent," Rottier said with a smile that looked closer to a grimace than an expression of satisfaction. "Perhaps you could give us an idea of what someone in your position would expect for his wisdom and involvement."

"Unfortunately," David replied, draining his tea, "the value of my integrity as a trusted servant of the sultan is far greater than the price of my perfidy. I am here, as I stated, to observe the enactment of the Tanzimat reforms and not to get involved in matters of commercial bigotry. Please understand, gentlemen, that the Jews are citizens of the Ottoman Empire. You are not. You are representatives of your own countries, and while you enjoy diplomatic freedom, I don't believe that includes the harassment of any of the sultan's subjects. And now that I have discerned the purpose of your invitation, I shall take my leave."

The consuls, their mouths open in disbelief, watched as David turned around and walked out. "What a rude bastard," said Wilkinson.

"The very worst," agreed Massi. "We shall have to watch him carefully."

Both Eskender and Sha were surprised to see David back so early. When they'd helped him take off his uniform and Sha had rustled up a simple dinner accompanied by wine, David filled them in.

"It's a great shame you are not a genuine *Reis ül-küttab,* effendi," said Eskender. "I think the Empire might be better served by men who think like you."

"You flatter me," David replied with a laugh. "But then again, you don't know everything about me. I wear some things on my sleeve and keep others in my heart. Now, what can you tell me about the local legends?"

THE GOLEM

Chapter 22

"I fear that I may disappoint you, effendi," Eskender said. "After I failed to discover anything related to cryptids in the market, I turned to some books in the library of one of the *kadis*. It contained the stories of the usual mythical and legendary monsters from their ancient texts. No one, of course, believes they are still around, and none seemed suitable for what you have in mind. Although I have no idea what that is." His face, normally impassive, gave nothing away.

"Well put," David said with a grin. "But you found something that you feel might be of interest to a man like me, whose motives are unknown but assumed to be pure and lawful?"

"I did." He took out a piece of paper and showed David a rough drawing of a plate that he'd found in one of the books. "This is Cronus, the leader of the Titans. He holds in his hand a *harpe*, a blade with a shape that may be familiar to you."

David scratched his chin as he examined the drawing of the seated Titan holding a curved dagger that looked, while not identical, quite similar to the *sica* that rested in its soft leather sheath on his left leg.

"And how did this Titan, Cronus, use this blade?"

"Legend has it that he used it to castrate Uranus, his father."

"Ha, a lesson for every parent not to leave blades lying about." David was about to add to the joke (which hadn't drawn a reaction from either Eskender or Sha) with a reference to the eunuch Amrani Lahlou but thought better of it. While both had said they reported to Reşid Pasha and not his de-testicled sidekick, he wasn't confident that he fully understood their relationship to the eunuch.

"Well, I am most certainly not disappointed in you, Eskender, though I do not as yet see how this information helps. I will think on it."

"Of course, effendi. One thing I do know is that the common people of Rhodes are a superstitious lot. Perhaps not more so than peasants from other countries, but susceptible to the things they don't understand. They see monsters when educated people see rational explanations."

"As do we all, Eskender. We all fear the unknown and the unknowable even more. It is this fear that makes us do irrational things, things we instinctively know are wrong."

"I'm not sure I understand, effendi. You have obviously dwelt upon this subject. Perhaps you can enlighten me."

"Eskender, for someone whose intelligence far exceeds most, you come across as quite naïve, and I must admit it puzzles me."

"My apologies, effendi. That is not my intent. I know I have great knowledge of the practical, but I have never known anyone willing to discuss the more philosophical nature of things with me. I sincerely value your thoughts."

"Is that so? Well, I am not a teacher or, for that matter, a philosopher, but I do think about the transcendent. It helps me to understand my own purpose. But very well, let me give you an example. No person capable of rational thought can think that it is right to own a slave. And yet many do, because they believe some higher power, whom they have not seen or spoken to or heard from directly but only by way of books written by self-professed experts, tells them it is permissible to possess another human being. To me, that is using the divine to justify something inherently wrong. Do you think the consuls knew that what they were encouraging the ex-governor to do to the Jews was wrong? Of course they did. But they did it anyway because their leaders—religious, political, or economic—have convinced them that Jewish ethnicity is fundamentally evil and must be destroyed."

Both Eskender and Sha looked at David with wide eyes as the man they'd thought of as calm and thoughtful seemed to become more riled by the moment. They didn't realize that it was, for the most part, a façade. David was certainly angry at the morally depleted consuls. Still, he was no stranger to hatred, and what the European representatives had done was no more or less hateful than many acts he'd witnessed over the years. In essence, what he was attempting to do was instill an apprehensiveness in both Sha and Eskender as to what he was capable of.

"I know you have been told more about me than I would, under normal circumstances, be comfortable with. Now I am going to expose the true extent of my proficiency. I am going to unleash a storm of death and destruction on those who have been judged by Reşid Pasha and the sultan himself to have committed crimes against citizens of the Empire."

"We will help you in any possible way, effendi," Sha said.

"No, I don't want your help . . . what? Have I upset you?"

"It seems you do not trust us," said Eskender.

"On the contrary. As I said, you know more about me and what I do than any living soul but my wife. What happens after this, however, is something I must do alone. Your involvement, as I made clear to the eunuch, compromises all of us."

"But effendi—"

"Sha, I am not your master. If anything, I am your friend, and as your friend, I will not risk your life or Eskender's. If you really want to help me, stay out of my way. Now, I am going to bed."

"Would you like me to join you?" asked Sha.

"Not tonight," David responded with a degree of regret that was hard to hide. He needed to be alone tonight because it seemed as good a night as any to do a practice run. When he was sure that both Eskender and Sha were in their rooms, he put on his darkest robe, wrapped a scarf around his face, and strapped on the *sica*. Then he opened the front door quietly and vanished into the night, heading towards the home of Wilkinson.

Chapter 23

The streets were mostly empty with only the occasional drunk staggering home from the taverns, which, if not already closed, were in the process of shutting down for the night.

David kept to the shadows, thankful that the waning moon was no more than a sliver. Close to Wilkinson's house was a building site which, at first, David ignored. Then he had an idea and looked around till he found a mound of hardening gypsum, which he knew was used to hold bricks together. He picked up a handful and, working quickly, molded it into a crude figure. This he placed in a pocket in his robe.

As he approached Wilkinson's house, he could see that the oil lamps still burned, and as he got closer, he could hear voices, though the words were indistinct. He watched from an alley, not sure how long to wait to see if there were still any consuls inside or if the sounds were from the servants cleaning up. Just as he thought it had to be the latter, the door to Wilkinson's house opened, and the French consul, Rottier, appeared with Wilkinson.

Much to David's surprise, the two consuls embraced each other, and Rottier kissed Wilkinson on the lips. It was not an affectionate peck but more of a languid romantic kiss. *Interesting*, David thought. *Clearly, you cannot judge a man's sensitivity by the brutality of his deeds.* He'd spent little time with Rottier earlier that evening, but he'd had more time with Wilkinson, and he'd never have pegged the man as homosexual. Not that it mattered or changed anything. He'd been hired to assassinate the consuls for what they'd done, not for what they were.

He followed the consul down the deserted street, making sure to stay out of sight even though the man's gait suggested that he was drunk and wouldn't have noticed David even if he were walking directly behind him. Rottier staggered along the dark street, emitting a sound that could equally have been interpreted as moaning as it could singing. After a block or two, he came to an alley. He turned in and, after a few steps, leaned up against a wall and began to fiddle with the buttons on the front flap of his trousers. He struggled at first, cursing loudly, until finally the flap fell and he was able to retrieve his penis. He peed against the wall, mumbling in relief.

As he finished and both hands were involved in returning his drained appendage to his pants, David stepped up behind him and, without a word, drove the *sica* into Rottier's left kidney, drawing it across to sever the renal artery. Rottier squeaked in pain and tried to turn round, but David held his head to the wall until he was satisfied that sufficient blood had spurted from the wound to ensure death. Then he wiped the *sica* on Rottier's shirt and returned it to the sheath strapped to his left leg.

He undid the strings to Rottier's purse so that, at the very least, his death would look like the result of a robbery and hastily put it in the pocket of his robe. He'd dispose of it later. The last thing he did was remove the little clay golem from his robe and place it next to the body. Then, looking around quickly to make sure the alley was clear, he stepped back onto the street and took a circuitous route back to his house in case he was being followed. He waited behind a tree near the front door of the house, and when he was satisfied that no one had followed him, he went inside and climbed into bed.

While no one had followed David home, the killing of Rottier had been witnessed by a figure also dressed in black. When the figure was certain that David had gone, he stepped up to Rottier's corpse as he'd been instructed and sliced off Rottier's scrotum. Then he carved the letter "G" into the dead man's cheek and tossed the scrotum down a drain. He searched in vain for Rottier's purse.

Eskender woke David with a cup of sweet, rich coffee, and as David sat up, Eskender looked over to where David's dark blue robe lay crumpled on the floor.

"Shall I ask Sha to clean that for you, effendi?" There was no disguising the suspicion in his voice.

"It is perfectly clean, thank you. And yes, in answer to your next unasked question, I did go out for a short walk to clear my head and consider my next move as it relates to the consuls."

Eskender bowed. "Of course, effendi. May I ask Sha to prepare you some food? And while she is in the kitchen, we can speak about what you wish to do today."

As David finished the last of the figs and *straggisto*, a messenger arrived to say that the temporary governor requested his presence as soon as possible to discuss an urgent matter. David was sure he knew what the governor wanted to discuss, and in this, he was not wrong.

"My dear *Reis ül-küttab*," said the temporary governor when David was shown into his office. "This is terrible, terrible." He had a large silk handkerchief in his right hand, which he used to mop the sweat that pooled on his forehead and bulbous cheeks.

"Governor, please," David said, trying to sound calm and in command, though he felt neither. "What is it . . . what is so terrible?"

"The French consul, Monsieur Rottier, has been murdered."

"Murdered, you say? But how? I was with him and the other consuls at Wilkinson's house just last evening, and despite having imbibed what appeared to me to be vast quantities of alcohol, he and the others were in good health. I left early."

"Yes, so I am told by the servants. They said that Rottier left Wilkinson's house in the early hours of this morning and was, as you said, highly intoxicated. It was then, on his way home, that someone stabbed him in a dark alley and . . .." He lowered his voice, and in a whisper that David could hardly hear, said, "And removed his genitals."

It was David's turn to sound alarmed. "Removed his genitals? By the beard of the Prophet, that is unspeakable." His mind began to race, and he immediately thought of what Eskender had told him of how the Titan, Cronus, had castrated his father, Uranus. Could Eskender have followed him and removed the consul's genitals after David had left? But why, and how had he gotten back to the house before David? It was impossible.

"Have you had the opportunity to investigate this terrible crime? Are there witnesses? Have you established a motive?" David asked, looking as stern as he imagined an Ottoman official would look.

"Our chief *kadi* has organized an inquiry, but as of an hour ago, he had found no witnesses. Rottier's purse was missing, and so the *kadi* believes it was robbery."

"So, nothing else was missing?"

"You mean other than his balls?"

"Of course I mean other than his balls. Was he carrying important documents?"

"Wilkinson and the servants say no. However, there is something else you should know: he had a strange symbol carved into his cheek. One of the *kadis* who is familiar with the Hebrew text says it could be what the Jews call *Gimel*, the letter 'G.' The doctor who examined the body said it was deliberately carved after death when the blood had already left the body."

David turned from the governor so that he wouldn't see him close his eyes. He took several short breaths until he was satisfied that his heart had stopped racing. Then he turned around.

"Who knows of Rottier's death?"

"So far, we have managed to contain the news, *Reis ül-küttab*. Other than the watchman who found the body, the two police officers who brought it to the jail for examination, the doctor and the *kadi* who examined it and made the identification, me, Wilkinson (who has agreed not to inform the other consuls just yet), and you. No one else."

Except for the castrator, he thought to himself. "Well, I suppose that is the best we can hope for. As this is a matter that ultimately affects the Sublime Porte, I must examine the body and the scene of the crime. Make sure it is sealed off, and perhaps you can have someone take me to the jail. And while you're at it, I would like Eskender to attend me there."

"Of course, *Reis ül-küttab*. And would you like me to round up some Jews?"

"Why would you do that?"

"Well, due to the *Gimel*, Wilkinson believes this has to be a revenge killing on their behalf. Jews are always after money, and perhaps the scrotum will be used as a ritual purse."

"Be very wary, Governor. Your predecessor allowed himself to be influenced by the consuls, and look where his weakness landed him. Your governorship is not yet confirmed, and after what you have just said, it now hangs on a thread thinner than the hair on a camel's tail. Before you do anything you will regret, let me examine the body and draw my own conclusions."

"Of course, *Reis ül-küttab*. One last thing: you asked what was missing."

"Yes," David replied impatiently.

"But you never asked if we found anything strange near the body?"

"And did you?"

The Governor reached into a drawer on his desk and withdrew a small clay figure. "We found this." He handed the figurine to David.

"Hmm," said David, examining the object. "It looks like some sort of statue. A talisman, perhaps . . . a pagan symbol?"

"It's not something I recognize, *Reis ül-küttab*. I was hoping a man of learning such as yourself might know."

"If I may interject, effendis," Eskender said, stepping up to the desk. He took the clay figure and looked at it thoughtfully. "I believe this is the symbol of the Melas Cult, named for the son of Poseidon."

"And what is this Melas Cult?"

"Supposedly, it is a group sworn to unite the Dodecanese Islands and return them from the Ottomans to the Hellenic Kingdom. This is hearsay, as very little has ever been written down about them."

"Well, this is startling news," the governor said, retrieving the clay figure from Eskender and examining it closely. "This cult is unknown to me, but be assured, *Reis ül-küttab,* I shall not rest until I find out more."

"See that you don't. Now, I have a body to examine."

Chapter 24

The underground room that served as the morgue was down a flight of rickety steps and next to a storeroom that held provisions for the prisoners. It was cooler than the offices and cells on the ground floor, but judging by the smell, not cold enough to stop a body from rotting. Both David and Eskender had to cover their faces with cloths soaked in camphor that the doctor provided.

The first thing David saw when the doctor pulled the sheet back was the very distinctive "G" carved into Rottier's cheek.

"What do you make of it, Eskender?" he said, watching the young man carefully to see if he had any reaction.

"It is most definitely a Hebrew *Gimel*, effendi. But what the significance is, I don't know."

"Really?" asked David. "You don't know . . . and what of the removal of the consul's genitals? Do you have an opinion on that?"

Eskender shook his head. "I don't, effendi. My opinion would be nothing more than an opinion." He bowed his head because he knew precisely what David was thinking.

"The interesting thing is," the doctor said, breaking the tension he hadn't picked up on, "I believe the removal of the consul's scrotum happened some time after he was stabbed in the kidneys. According to the police officer who removed the body, there was a great deal of blood where the initial kidney stab would have occurred but very little where his balls used to be. The same goes for the cut on his face. You'll notice virtually no blood on his cheek."

"And your conclusion, my dear doctor?" David asked, already knowing the answer.

"There were two separate assailants. First, the kidney slasher, followed a short time later by the ball remover and cheek carver. And by the way, just as a matter of interest, the scrotum must have been carried away—for what purpose, I don't even want to contemplate."

David gave an inward sigh. That was the last thing he wanted to hear. If the consuls knew that the scrotum had been carried off, they'd immediately claim, like the governor, that it was the Jews again using it for some ritualistic purpose.

"Before we jump to conclusions, doctor, I am going to examine the scene of the crime. Eskender, I'd like you to accompany me. And doctor, did you know about the clay talisman found beside the body?" David asked.

"I was informed about it, *Reis ül-küttab*, but I put it down to a child's toy abandoned in the same spot. Pure coincidence, I believe."

One of the policemen agreed to show them to the crime scene, though, of course, David knew the location. It was no more than a ten-minute walk from the police station, and he and Eskender walked a few steps behind the officer. Before David could say anything, Eskender placed his hand on David's arm.

"I know what is on your mind, effendi, and I swear on my mother's soul that neither Sha nor I had anything to do with it. Both of us heard you go out, but your instructions were clear that we were not to get involved, and so we didn't."

"I want to believe you, Eskender, but you must agree that there are peculiar coincidences. You were the one who told me of the Titan removing his father's scrotum and the letter 'G.' Forgive my doubt, but that could well stand for 'golem.' I'm certain Reşid Pasha revealed that this is my codename for this operation."

"You are correct about the legend of the Titan, effendi, but I know nothing of this 'golem.'" There was no hesitation in his voice, no hint of deceit, and so, somewhat reluctantly, David was forced to believe him.

"And the Melas Cult?"

"That I made up, effendi. I failed at your request to discover any pagan beliefs of the island, so I invented one."

"Brilliant, Eskender. Quite brilliant. It was I who placed the figurine near the body, and I will tell you why later." He patted Eskender on the back.

The crime scene had been secured by two policemen who stood guard with long staves, which they used to hold back some stray dogs who were sniffing around the dried blood. Passersby appeared totally uninterested and barely acknowledged the policemen, who in turn barely acknowledged David and Eskender.

"The doctor is correct, as I'm sure you already suspect. There was another man." David surveyed the scene carefully, though he didn't expect to find anything. "The questions are, who sliced off his genitals and carved the 'G,' and for what purpose?"

"Most importantly, effendi, do you think whoever this person is saw you?"

"I took great pains to cover my face, and I was extremely careful when I left our house and when I returned. So even if this person saw me kill Rottier, I am quite certain he didn't know it was me. But let me ask you this, Eskender: why do you think they severed his balls? Was it to make a statement, perhaps about his sexual proclivity?"

"His sexual proclivity, effendi?"

"Ah, yes. Well, I failed to tell you that while I was watching Wilkinson's house, I saw him and Rottier in an embrace that suggested something more than casual friendship."

Before Eskender could respond, he was interrupted by one of the policemen, who swung his stave at two dogs who'd been pawing at the drain opposite where the body was found. Eskender walked over to the drain and crouched down. Then he stuck his hand in and removed an object that he brought over to David.

It was covered in waste, but the hairs and wrinkles on the sack-like object made it crystal clear to David that Eskender held Rottier's scrotum.

Chapter 25

The governor shrieked as David dropped Rottier's scrotum on his desk next to his half-finished cup of coffee. A blob that could have been a testicle or a piece of debris from the drain rolled out and splattered on the floor.

"This," said David, "is Rottier's ball sack as identified by the doctor and found in a drain at the scene of the crime. It was not, as you suggested, carried off by the Jews for some ritual. So now what do you have to say for yourself?"

The governor looked as if he were about to vomit. "Perhaps I was hasty in agreeing with Wilkinson. I shall tell him of your findings at once, *Reis ül-küttab*."

"Yes, do that, and perhaps also ask him if he can think of another reason someone should have sliced off Rottier's balls?"

"I fail to understand . . . ."

"I'm sure you do not understand, but Wilkinson most certainly will. Now, I have been notified that I am expected back in Constantinople within the next few days. An unfortunate incident has occurred in another of the Empire's provinces that Reşid Pasha says requires my attention. I must warn you that if anything should befall the Jewish community of Rhodes after I leave, you will pay a heavy price."

Wilkinson understood perfectly, but not for the reason David suspected. "Get this thing away from me," he said to the governor, who'd had the one-teste-less object transferred from his desk to a ceramic bowl. They were sitting in Wilkinson's study because the governor had no faith that the servants and staff at the governor's residence could resist eavesdropping. He'd gone as soon as David had left his office.

"Why in God's name did your man decide to leave this at the crime scene? It may have ruined everything. He was supposed to carry it away with him."

"I know, I know," the governor replied, wringing his hands. "Good help is difficult to find. I'd promised him he could keep Rottier's purse, but it was missing, and so I imagine he lost interest in the assignment after that. But don't worry: he is safely aboard a ship heading for Mykonos, and of course, he won't make it. The other thing is that the doctor believes someone else killed Rottier."

Wilkinson looked as if he was about to explode. "What? What in God's name do you mean?"

"Well, the doctor believes that Rottier was killed a while before our man removed his scrotum and carved the 'G' on his face."

"And did your man tell you that?"

"Um, no. He failed to mention that when he reported to me. I'd ask him, but I fear he may be at the bottom of the sea already. The boat he was on sailed at six o'clock this morning."

Wilkinson had transitioned from apoplexy to hand-wringing. "This is terrible news. Another killer."

"I would not be too concerned," said the governor. "The killer was no doubt a thief who took Rottier's purse."

"Perhaps, but what happens if he's not? Don't forget von Königsmark died under mysterious circumstances, and our colleague in Constantinople warned us that someone has been sent by Ręsid Pasha himself. Whoever that is may well be a killer."

"The pasha refers to the *Reis ül-küttab*. Not some random murderer. I assure you, his interest is in our application of the Tanzimat reforms and the treatment of the Jews under the reforms. I doubt he even knows our connection to the sponge trade. In any case, he indicated that he must return to Constantinople in a day or two. Apparently, Ręsid Pasha has another task for him."

"I don't like him, and I most certainly don't trust him. Seems the complete opposite of an Ottoman official. Too righteous. Not open to anything."

"Are you saying I am?"

"No, I don't need to say it. You're as crooked as a ram's horn, governor, but then so am I."

The governor laughed. "It's good that someone did our work for us, but what about von Sturmer and Massi? It's going to look very suspicious if they both die now, what with von Königsmark's rather mysterious demise."

"You're right, they can't die. Rather, they must be seen to disappear, as if they have been reassigned."

"We won't be able to blame the Jews, unfortunately. Your idea of removing Rottier's testicles and carving the 'G' for 'goy' on his cheek did not really work. And to be honest, I got the impression from the *Reis ül-küttab* that he believed that Rottier's balls were removed for a totally different reason. He said you'd know what he meant."

Wilkinson gave a dismissive wave. "What nonsense! Why would I know what he meant?"

"Well, I make no judgment. Of course, the Koran forbids it, but it was well known that Rottier took a delight in the company of men rather than women."

"And why would I know anything about it?"

The governor detected a weakening in Wilkinson's bravado and decided to twist the dagger. He was a little tired of the Englishman's arrogance.

"Personally, I don't care about the intimate actions of others, but the *Reis ül-küttab* mentioned it, and so I bring it up, whether as a warning to be cautious or simply a warning against flouting the laws of the Koran. You decide. But come, let us forget this and instead discuss how we will ensure that our two colleagues vanish before they find out exactly what we have discovered. I certainly don't want to share my proceeds with them." He smiled to himself as the blood drained from Wilkinson's face.

"Urr," went Wilkinson, sounding like the deflating bladder of a sheep. "I thought perhaps they should receive some correspondence from Damascus or somewhere within their territory to attend some kind of event, and they could somehow vanish on the journey, either on the ship or in an attack by brigands. After all, despite the British, Austrian, and Russian forces helping your new young Sultan Abdülmecid, there are bands of mercenaries wandering the territory who are still loyal to the Khedive of Egypt. I'm sure with your contacts, you can arrange an unfortunate accident."

"Accidents can always be arranged. The question is, why would they go, and equally importantly, why would you not? After all, Britain is leading the expedition."

"Let me think upon it," Wilkinson said. "I will let you know tomorrow."

As soon as the governor left, Wilkinson opened the screen door that led from his study to a secret suite of rooms known only to him and a select group of servants who'd been paid handsomely to keep their mouths shut.

"What do you think, Amrani Lahlou?" he asked the eunuch, who sat like a fat, contented cat on a cushion, eating candied walnuts and drinking sherbet.

"I think you are a very good actor, Mr. Wilkinson. Your fear and confusion were most convincing. You and the governor, however, made a stupid mistake by hiring a man to sever the testicles of Rottier and carve the 'G' into his cheek in the hope that the Jews would be blamed. All you had to do was wait for the sultan's assassin to kill the other consuls as he would have done, and then you could have accused the Jews of a revenge killing."

"But he may have killed me as well."

"Yes, he may have, and I still might allow that to happen if the fool of a governor even suspects that you and

I are the real partners in this discovery. Like him, I don't intend to share my portion with anyone else."

Chapter 26

"What happens now, effendi?" asked Eskender as he, Sha, and David sat around the kitchen table drinking tea. "It seems as if you may have to rethink your plans."

"The only change is to the timeline. I must complete my mission within the next day or so, and then we must leave."

"I don't wish to be presumptuous," Sha said, putting her hand on David's and then immediately withdrawing it as if she'd done so in error, "but that seems like an excessive and even more dangerous undertaking, even for someone as accomplished as you."

David laughed. "I appreciate the compliment. Yes, it is certainly precarious and maybe even extreme, but I don't believe it will be impossible. Eskender came up with a quick-witted and ingenious idea in front of the governor, which, if I am lucky, will give me the time I need."

Eskender explained the Melas Cult idea to Sha, who, judging by her expression, was not quite as enthusiastic as David.

"Both of you know from Reşid Pasha that my trade-name is The Golem—at least that's what I told the pasha and the sultan."

"And what is a 'golem?'" asked Sha.

"A mythical creature fashioned from mud by a rabbi whose job it is to destroy those who harm Jews. The most famous one was made by a rabbi from Prague when the Jews were accused of a crime similar to the ones that led to the tragic events here in Rhodes."

"How very appropriate," Sha said.

"Last night, I decided to leave a small clay figure by the body, a figure that resembled the golem. I plan to leave one by each body to give the impression that the killings are purposeful and carried out by a practitioner of cult executions who leaves his mark. Eskender's story of the Melas Cult fits perfectly with that. If I am lucky, the governor, who is a fool, will spend his time trying to find members of this cult to blame. Now, what I need from you, Eskender, is to arrange a meeting tonight with Massi, the Swedish consul, and von Sturmer, the Austrian. It should be discreet and must take place after dark."

"You're in luck," Sha said. "The moon will be gone by tonight. But your logic escapes me. Even if you are discreet, when the two vice-consuls meet the same fate as their colleague, you could easily come under suspicion."

"I am in a position that is above suspicion. No one in their right mind would accuse the agent of Reşid Pasha and the sultan himself of murder. There will always be someone else, a lesser being, to pin the blame on, just as the consuls found Istamboli to accuse of the boy's murder.

It slipped my mind until his name came up, but the rabbi mentioned during our visit that cloaked men had broken into Istamboli's house while he was being held in jail. I meant to ask you to see if you could uncover the reason, Eskender."

"I shall do my best once I've set up the meeting, effendi."

"Thank you. Now, once again, I must ask you to trust me on this. At no time during my career have I been as forthcoming as I have with you two, not even with my wife. It goes against everything my father taught me about the silence and secrets of the assassin's trade."

Eskender stood up. "I understand, effendi. I shall go to arrange the meeting. What about Wilkinson, should they enquire?"

"Tell them I am meeting with him separately. My feeling is they will relish the idea of meeting with me alone. There is no honor amongst thieves, and I suspect they all distrust each other."

While Eskender went to arrange the meeting with the two consuls, Sha gave David another lesson in the ways Circassian warriors prepared for battle. An hour later, feeling relaxed and yet enthusiastic for what lay ahead, he met Eskender in the kitchen.

"You were right, effendi. Both Massi and von Sturmer are most keen to meet with you. It is arranged for ten o'clock at Massi's house. May I assume you don't wish me to accompany you?"

"On the contrary, I would like you to accompany me. I need a witness."

Eskender hesitated. "I am loyal to you, effendi, but—"

"Don't worry, Eskender. I don't need you to witness their deaths. I need you to witness what I believe we will discover at Massi's house at that hour. Now, I think I will walk over to the governor's house to say my farewells. Sha, if you wouldn't mind packing our meager possessions, and Eskender, you will need to go to the docks to arrange our passage. Be sure we're on the first ship out of here in the morning."

As Eskender left and Sha gathered their belongings, David slipped out. He donned his simple white robes and slid the *sica* into its scabbard attached to his left ankle before setting out to the building site, where he found that the gypsum from the previous evening had not yet hardened. The workmen had gone for the night, and he was able to grab enough to fashion two small golems without anyone seeing him. Then he made his way over to the market, where he bought a small saddle bag and a black robe, which the storekeeper allowed him to try on in the back of the store.

"Perfect," he said to the storekeeper. "I'll tuck this old robe of mine in the saddle bag and take it home to my wife to wash. She'll be most impressed with the black one, which won't show the dirt." The storekeeper, who couldn't have cared less why David wanted a new robe but was secretly pleased that the customer hadn't even tried to bargain with him, smiled and wished David a good evening.

There was still too much daylight for what David had in mind for the consuls, and so he bought a pastry and a small glass of mint tea from a vendor and sat on a wall overlooking Mandraki Harbor and stared at the Castle of Saint Nickolaus.

He thought of what he and Sha had done that afternoon, and that conjured an image of his wife, Ruth, and he wondered what she was doing at this time back in Baghdad. She was probably feeding the children and telling them that their father would be home soon. He recalled what Sha had said the first time they'd had sex: that he wasn't David Smulian-Hasson, husband of Ruth, at that moment, but instead the *Reis ül-küttab*, envoy of the sultan, and that his conscience should be clear. But it wasn't, and he knew he'd betrayed Ruth, for which there could be no forgiveness.

In the distance, he thought he saw Eskender talking to someone next to a large sailing vessel, and he assumed arrangements for the next day's travel were being negotiated. He took a bite of the phyllo and walnut pastry, and the aroma of honey and cinnamon took him back to Sha, to the place between her thighs that was as sweet as any pastry he'd ever tasted, and he knew he could never confess his transgressions to Ruth. The job would be completed, and Sha and Eskender would return to Constantinople while he set sail for Baghdad. Ruth never asked for details about his assignments, and he never offered them up. The amount of money in the chest that Sha kept would ensure that his family had more than enough to live on, even if he never worked again. The problem, he realized, was not in confessing to Ruth but in saying goodbye to Sha. His mind whirled for a moment, but then the discipline of a thousand years of Smulian assassins kicked in, and his focus turned once again to the task at hand.

He finished the pastry, returned the empty tea glass to the vendor, and pulled the loose cloth of the headpiece around his face. As the sun disappeared below the Aegean, turning the sky a dark purple, he began to walk towards the house of Massi. It was two hours until the arranged meeting, plenty of time to accomplish his carefully constructed plan.

Chapter 27

The streets on which the wealthy residents of Rhodes lived were set away from the hustle of the commercial thoroughfares. The sliver of moon from two nights ago had vanished, and the only barriers to Massi's house for the now-focused assassin from Baghdad were a high wall and a tall metal gate guarded by a large man with a cudgel.

It wasn't the first time that David had encountered seemingly impossible obstacles. There was no doubt in his mind that he could have easily dispatched the guard, but he needed him to stay alive to swear, at some point in the future, that no one had entered the house before David's scheduled arrival. He wondered about servants but decided Massi would have sent them home by this time.

There was a large olive tree that hung over a slightly lower wall at a house two down from Massi's. It looked easy enough to climb, and so long as there was no one in the yard of the house to catch him and a branch didn't snap to alert the guard, he could safely make his way to Massi's abode. At that moment, the guard was focused on a flask of something that David did not believe was coffee, so he felt safe to proceed.

The tree proved more difficult to climb than David had anticipated. He put that down to the fact that he hadn't climbed one in over ten years, nor had he had much exercise since the horse journey from Baghdad to Alexandretta in the company of *Boluk-bashi* Fidan. His ascent was neither nimble nor silent, but he did the job without arousing any attention.

David crept along the walls of the two residences adjacent to Massi's till he came to the higher wall of the consul's house. He lay prone on top of the wall and observed the courtyard and small garden that surrounded the house. It was dark except for a light that emanated from a room on the first floor, and the only way to access that room, assuming the ground-floor doors were locked, was yet another tree whose lower branches were no more than two feet from the latticed balcony. David climbed from the wall onto the tree and got as close to the lattice as he could to see if there was a gap he could squeeze through or a panel that slid open.

From behind the lattice, he could hear the murmur of voices, and through the slats, he saw Massi and von Sturmer sitting at a table drinking wine. A single candle burned in a holder, and a pepperbox revolver lay near Massi's glass. David's foot slipped, and a small branch snapped. Both men looked up and Massi grabbed his gun. They waited a few seconds and then cautiously made their way to the balcony. David knew any movement would give him away, and the only hope he had was that the tree would conceal his bulk. He held his breath as the two men peered through the slats.

"I don't see anything," von Sturmer said as Massi opened a section of the lattice. To David's relief, Massi looked down rather than at the tree.

"There's nothing down there. Probably a cat or rodent. You're on edge, von Sturmer."

"I'm on edge? You're the one with your finger on the trigger of the pepperbox. As much as I cannot abide the *Reis ül-küttab*, I'm glad we're meeting with him rather than Wilkinson. That English swine has mischief in mind. I feel it in my bones."

"Your bones? Good God, man. You're like an old woman. Control your feelings before they ruin everything."

Von Sturmer clenched his fists, and David thought he might take a swing at the Swede. Massi closed the section of lattice he'd opened, and the two men turned and walked back from the balcony into the room, where they continued to drink wine and talk.

David strained to hear what they were saying. The conversation about Wilkinson intrigued him. He'd sensed mistrust in the way the other consuls viewed Wilkinson on the night of the dinner, and now his suspicions were confirmed.

He edged forward as carefully as he could, testing the branch with every inch, and then, to his relief, he found that Massi had not locked the lattice opening. As he began to calculate whether he could push it open and launch himself onto the balcony and into the room before Massi could aim and fire the pepperbox, Massi stood up and walked out of the room. Von Sturmer poured himself another glass of wine and then took a document from his coat pocket and began to read. As he moved the candle closer to where he sat to illuminate the document, David made his move.

He pushed open the screen as silently as he could and then fell forward onto the balcony, rolling into a ball. As he rolled, his right hand went to his left ankle, and by the time he'd sprung to his feet inches from where von Sturmer sat, the *sica* was primed to kill. The Austrian was so startled by the apparition that sprang up in front of him that he froze. As he opened his mouth to scream, David grabbed the back of his neck and pulled him forward till he lay across the table. Then, before von Sturmer could recover whatever of his wits remained, David plunged the *sica* into his right kidney and drew it across, severing the renal artery. Von Sturmer gave a pitiful whimper and slumped down from where he lay across the table onto the floor, his life dissolving in a dark pool of blood.

There was no time to drag the body away from the table, so David stayed in the shadows to the right of the door as he heard Massi climbing the stairs. Massi stopped, and David thought he heard him sniffing the air as if he could smell blood and death, which didn't surprise David as there was a copious amount of blood and von Sturmer had voided his bowels as he died. Then Massi burst into the room, swinging the pepperbox from side to side. He glanced down at von Sturmer's corpse for an instant, but it was all the time David needed. He went into a crouch and delivered the numbing blow to Massi's sciatic nerve. It was the first part of the non-lethal move all Smulian-Hasson assassins learned and was normally followed up by a sharp, incapacitating blow to the jugular.

Massi fell to the floor, writhing in agony. He dropped the pepperbox and David kicked it away. Massi attempted to sit up, but the pain was too great, and he vomited a foul-smelling mixture of wine and whatever food he and von Sturmer had eaten earlier. Before he could move again, David knelt on his back and pushed Massi's head into the vomit. He forced Massi's left arm halfway up his back till he knew the slightest of movements would dislocate the shoulder and placed the tip of the *sica* just under Massi's right eye.

"Now," he said, "If you don't wish to suffer further pain, you will tell me why you are plotting against Wilkinson."

"Who are you?" groaned Massi

"I am The Golem," David said. "That is all you need to know. Now answer my question, and I will make the pain go away."

"Please," said Massi, trying to turn his head further from the vomit. "We think Wilkinson is in league with a high official in the Sublime Porte and is working to eliminate us. I do not know this official's name. Only that Wilkinson calls him 'Nutless.'"

"What does that mean?" David pushed the tip of the *sica* into Massi's flesh.

"I swear by the Blessed Virgin that is all I know. "

It was clear to David that Massi was telling the truth. He was a coward, and cowards, in David's experience, will tell their interrogators anything and everything to avoid further pain.

"Very well," David said, removing the *sica* from Massi's face. "I believe you."

"Wait!" Massi twisted his head so he could see David's face. "I know you . . . you are the *Reis ül-küttab.* Why are you doing this?"

"The sultan has decreed that anyone who unlawfully visits torture and false accusation against his subjects—whether Muslim, Christian, or Jew—must suffer the consequences. This is yours." He pushed the *sica* into Massi's left kidney and drew it across to sever the renal artery. This, the second and more dramatic shock to Massi's body, killed him instantly.

David took the two golem figurines out of the saddlebag and placed them next to each body. He wiped the blood off the *sica* and returned it to the scabbard on his left ankle. Then he climbed back through the lattice screen into the tree and made his way back along the wall to the first tree he'd climbed. The guard, still outside the gate to Massi's house, was blissfully unaware of the happenings in the house he guarded.

All of that changed an hour later when the *Reis ül-küttab* and his secretary, Eskender, arrived at Massi's house for their ten o'clock appointment. The guard showed them in as he'd been instructed and called from the bottom of the stairs for his master. When the vice-consul failed to respond, the guard excused himself to the visitors and slowly ascended the stairs. The scream he uttered when he came across the two bodies was higher-pitched than either David or Eskender was expecting from such a large man.

"Ya Allah," exclaimed the governor when he was shown the carnage in the upstairs room of Massi's house later that night. "Look, the figurines! It is that damn Melas Cult again."

"And have you made any progress in apprehending those brigands?" asked David. He and Eskender had reported the crime to the governor, explaining how they'd arrived at the gory scene for their meeting. They'd then accompanied him, a judge, and three policemen back to Massi's house to examine the killings. Eskender had not asked David how he'd managed to kill the two men without anyone seeing him.

"No, *Reis ül-küttab.* Unfortunately, we have made little progress with the Melas Cult; they must be skilled operators. The guard swears that no one came to the house between the time von Sturmer arrived and you and Eskender came for your meeting."

"He told us the same," said Eskender, "and I looked around the property. There doesn't appear to be any way in or out except through the front gate."

David shook his head. "This makes no sense. You must warn Wilkinson. He could be next."

"That may not be necessary. He informed me earlier tonight that he is leaving on the first tide for Acre to help draft the final negotiations between Britain and Muhammad Ali Pasha, the troublesome Khedive of Egypt."

"A pity," David said. "I was hoping to visit him again to say my goodbyes. Ah, well, it is late, and I am tired and must make final arrangements for my own departure later tomorrow."

After spending a few more minutes with the governor and promising to stop at the residence for a final farewell on his way to the harbor the following day if time permitted, David and Eskender left the scene of the double slaughter and began to walk home.

"Look, Eskender," he said as they turned onto the street where their house stood, "there is something I must do this night if I am to complete my mission."

"I understand perfectly, effendi. I assumed based on us leaving tomorrow that you'd need to finish the task tonight."

"To be honest, I planned to dispatch Wilkinson tomorrow morning just before we left. The governor may be dimwitted, and despite what I told you earlier about being above suspicion, even he will start to have his doubts if I draw this out too long. I want you to go back to the house and make sure everything is packed up and ready."

"It will be done, effendi. Sha has already taken care of most of it. The boat leaves tomorrow, probably at the same time as Wilkinson's, which means we will have to leave the house by the sixth hour. Will that give you enough time?"

"I don't know. I'm going to walk for a bit to think this through. Look, Eskender." He put his hand on the Ethiopian's shoulder. "I want you to listen very carefully and not question what I am going to say. If I don't make it to the ship on time, I want you and Sha to leave without me."

"We cannot do that, effendi. We were ordered to stay with you until you leave Rhodes. In any case, what about your money? We cannot keep what is yours."

"I cannot yet picture how to go about killing Wilkinson. The lack of a well-thought-out plan is a grave weakness in my profession. A hundred things could go wrong. If I don't make it, it is because I am dead, in which case you will be able to tell the pasha that you were with me until the end. As for the money, I would like you and Sha to take some—I will trust the amount to your honesty—and send the rest to my wife and children in Baghdad if you can. Promise me this."

Eskender put his hand on his heart. "As you will." He had no intention of abandoning David at this stage of their journey, but he could see there was no point in arguing. He touched David's arm in a gesture of friendship and began to walk towards the house. The gesture surprised David, but it also moved him.

David was troubled about the remainder of the mission. He had no idea how he'd get to Wilkinson before he left for Acre. Creating a plan without understanding the environment was a recipe for disaster. He'd had a vague notion that he'd visit Wilkinson on the way to the harbor the next morning under the pretext of saying goodbye, somehow complete his assignment, and board the ship before anyone discovered the dead British consul.

That in itself was a weak plan, but at least it was a plan. Tonight was just a jumble of thoughts with no clear picture. The news that Wilkinson was leaving on first tide threw everything into confusion. It meant that he'd have to get to Wilkinson's house far too early. Either the servants would have to wake Wilkinson, or the consul would be so busy making his final arrangements that he'd refuse the meeting. It couldn't possibly work. The other option was to break into the house in the next hour, just like he had at Massi's. But from what he remembered of the house, it was set back from the walls, and he doubted he could pull off the same stealthy entry.

To add a further complication, he'd left the saddle bag with the black robe at his own house when he went to get Eskender. Not for the first time that night, he worried about his own state of mind. Never in his whole career had he allowed outside distractions to cloud his focus on the job at hand, and yet here he was with little time left to complete the most important assassination of his life and no idea how to do it. He tried to free his mind of Sha and Ruth, but he failed each time.

He stopped walking when he came in sight of the harbor and stared out across the dark sea, trying desperately to draw inspiration from the black void. He was so focused on what was happening in his mind that he didn't see the two figures creeping silently out of the shadows until they were directly behind him. When he sensed their presence, it was already too late. He felt a sharp blow to the back of his head and then nothing.

When he woke up and realized where he was and who was in the room with him, he knew that he was already dead.

Chapter 28

His mouth was dry and his head ached, and what little light crept in from under the door at the top of the stairs into the cellar slowed his ability to fully comprehend his situation. He was in a wooden chair—that much was obvious—with his hands tied behind his back to the frame of the chair with a thin rope looping around his neck. The slightest motion of his arms or any rocking back and forth caused the rope to tighten across his throat. His inability to move, as terrifying as it was, helped to focus his mind, and as the cloudiness dissipated, he began to assess his predicament.

He could not feel any rope around his legs, and he managed to lift his right leg and feel for the *sica* on his left ankle. To his surprise and relief, it was still there. Either his captors hadn't thought to search in a relatively obscure place for a weapon, or they hadn't had time. He took deep breaths to slow his heart rate and began to assess his options. It took him no more than a few seconds to realize they were extremely limited. Even if he could dislodge the *sica* with his right foot, there was no way he could reach it.

The chair was flimsy, and the legs wobbled, but there was no slack in the rope.

Panic did not set in immediately, and he wondered how many of his ancestors had died in similar hopeless situations. The fact that the *sica* was still in the hands of a Smulian was evidence enough to suggest that he'd be the first one, and he felt a deep shame and sadness that he'd never be able to pass it on to his son. The panic, which had been pushed off to the side in the face of dismay, returned with a vengeance when the door at the top of the stairs opened and Wilkinson came down carrying a lantern.

"Aha," said the consul, holding the light in front of David's face, "the filthy Jew from Baghdad has returned to the land of the living, a state I'm afraid to say you won't be enjoying for very long."

"How dare you," David replied, doing his best to sound indignant, knowing full well that it wasn't going to mean a thing. "I am the *Reis ül-küttab*, appointed by the sultan himself. I demand you let me go."

Wilkinson smashed his fist into David's face, splitting his lip and loosening a tooth. David screwed his eyes in pain and watched as the consul danced around, shaking his hand in agony from the blow. "You swine, you may have broken my hand. I'll . . . I'll—"

"Save your threats, Wilkinson," whispered a figure from the doorway. The light from the lantern that Wilkinson had put on the floor while he rubbed his right fist failed to illuminate the intruder, who wobbled gingerly down the stairs. But the darkness did nothing to disguise the horror that erupted in David's brain. He felt his bowels churn and throat constrict. He needed no light to know exactly who it was that had entered the cellar. The shape of the body and the high-pitched voice were enough for him to know that whatever happened next was not going to be pleasant.

"I bid you good morning, Smulian-Hasson," said Amrani Lahlou, chief eunuch to Reşid Pasha, the second most powerful man in the Ottoman Empire. "I fear the deception is over."

"What deception?" David asked, trying his best not to swallow too much of the blood from his torn lip. "If there was deception, then you and your employer were part of it." He did not feel at all brave, but he saw the long knife that Lahlou held in his hand, and he knew he had to delay whatever diabolical torture the eunuch and the consul had planned for him.

"Well, that depends," Lahlou said. "True, I deceived Reşid Pasha and the young fool who calls himself the sultan and the other consuls whom you very conveniently eliminated before Wilkinson and I could take care of them. But I did not deceive my friend and colleague Mr. Wilkinson, who has been in on the plan all along."

"Your friend?" David asked, sounding as desperate as he felt. "The one who calls you 'Nutless?'"

"*Nutless?*" Lahlou looked at Wilkinson, his fat lip twisting into a sneer.

"Absolute bosh, old boy. He's making it up. Now you need to get on with it. I have a ship to catch, and I'd like to see this blaggard suffer before I do."

"My dear Wilkinson," said Lahlou, touching the tip of the long knife to his finger as if to test its sharpness, "torture is not something that can be rushed. Do you know it took my first master nearly two weeks to remove my sexual organs? I screamed for the first week and passed out for the second. But the great pleasure he took in making sure I did not bleed to death has remained with me. In the end, I would have done anything for him as the pain I felt and the pleasure he derived seemed to blend into one another. We do not have two weeks, unfortunately. If I am to retrieve the treasure today, then I have no more than a few hours. That should be sufficient, don't you agree?"

"You're the expert. I like inflicting pain as much as the next man, and believe me, I'd love to hang around for the show, but you'll have to do it without me. I can't afford to miss the ship to Acre, which sails within the hour."

"Go ahead. I'm perfectly capable on my own."

"Suit yourself. I'll leave the door open so I can hear his first scream. You can tell me all about it when we next meet. I'll stop by the governor's place and let him know that he can rest easy; the Melas Cult is no more. And Amrani, if you double-cross me, my son will kill you."

"Me? Double-cross you? My dear Wilkinson, have a little faith. No, the rest of the treasure will be waiting right here with your son. Do hurry back."

Wilkinson gave a chuckle and aimed a kick at David's shin. "Enjoy hell, you filthy Jew."

David winced in pain and knew that it was only going to get worse. He tried to think of a good retort to fling at Wilkinson but couldn't.

Chapter 29

"Well, well, Mr. Golem, where oh where should we begin?" Lahlou tapped a pudgy finger to his lips as if contemplating a meal rather than a torture session.

"That's your prerogative, but hurry up. I don't wish to be in your presence any longer than necessary, you bloated monstrosity." It was a dangerous game, but David knew that provoking the eunuch would lead to one of two actions. Either he would become so enraged he'd finish David off quickly, which would be preferable to a drawn-out session of unthinkable pain, or he'd strike David hard enough to topple the chair. The latter, David reasoned, might loosen his bonds if the rope didn't strangle him first. It was a long shot, but at this moment, it was all he had.

Lahlou laughed. "You seek to provoke me. However, you should understand that I have lived my life suffering the barbs and taunts of fools and bullies who feed their depleted souls with the discomfort of others. It will not work, Smulian-Hasson. I assure you that the pain you will suffer will bring me a relief as great as if I were having sex with a harem of virgins."

"I don't believe that."

"Let me explain. There are two types of eunuchs. The first have had only their testicles removed. Those are the ones who are put in charge of the harem because they feel no desire. The second have had their penises removed. Those are the ones whose sexual frustration is so intense, so fierce, because they can feel desire, but they cannot satisfy themselves. The only way they can rid themselves of the demon is to inflict pain on others." Lahlou undid his tunic until he stood naked in front of David. Then he lifted his belly, which hung down to his thighs, and revealed a shaved groin with only a small dark hole where his penis should have been. In the hole was a ruby the size of an apricot. David tried to look away, but he couldn't.

"If you're wondering why I have the ruby, it's a plug to stop my urine running out. I had it fashioned by a jeweler from a piece of the treasure that Wilkinson and I are in the process of removing from the house of the Jew Istamboli. I'll leave my tunic open so you can view it when you're suffering and imagine what I went through."

"I don't understand," David said, doing his best to avoid looking at the horrific sight.

"Of course you don't. Well, there is no harm in telling you now, I suppose. You won't be in a position to reveal any of it in an hour or so when I cut out your tongue. You see, Wilkinson is a bit of a classical scholar and archaeologist. An amateur to be sure, but he's constantly researching libraries and digging up sites on the island. A very English pastime, I am told. One of his obsessions was what became of the great treasure that the Knights Templar were forced to hand over to the Knights Hospitaller here in Rhodes when their order was disbanded. The treasure had vanished when the Ottomans defeated the Knights in 1522 and has remained thus—until a few months ago. That's when Wilkinson, burrowing like some starving dog for a buried bone, stumbled across the secret diary of Philippe Villiers de L'Isle-Adam, the last Grand Master of the Knights of Rhodes, before he and his motley group fled to Malta. It was there for all to see in the governor's library, but no one did. Except for Wilkinson, clever little worm that he is. It's a lengthy story, and honestly, I don't wish to waste any of the precious time I have left to make you suffer by regaling you with the details of how he deciphered the code that led to the treasure hidden behind a wall in Istamboli's house, which had once been a grain-storage structure for the castle. We got some of it out while the wretch was in prison, and as Istamboli conveniently died from his torture just a few days ago, I intend to remove the remaining items today with help from Wilkinson's son."

"So, everything was planned by you?"

"Yes, Wilkinson and I were already in business together. Then, after a night of heavy drinking, Wilkinson hinted to the other consuls about something that would make them all rich. We intended to get rid of them before we had to share any of the treasure, but then you very conveniently came into the picture and did the job for us. And all very legitimately, too. It's funny how life works, don't you think?"

"No, I don't. You killed, tortured, and starved an entire community just to get hold of some treasure?"

"Don't be sentimental; they were only Jews after all. Hardly a people to get upset over. Oh, I forgot—you're one, too." He gave a loud cackle, and David noticed a little dribble of urine around the edge of the ruby plug.

"You don't have to do this to me," David said. "I understand why Wilkinson might hate me for killing his friends, but I have not done anything to you other than carry out your pasha's orders. There is no reason for you to hate me. If I assassinate Wilkinson, then the treasure is all yours."

"Tempting, but Wilkinson won't be back for a week at least. No, Wilkinson is no longer your concern. I'll take care of him myself. And please understand, I don't hate you more than I hate any other man who has not suffered what I have. Believe me, I'd do the same to anyone else in your position. It's a need I have. Like an itch you cannot scratch. Hearing the screeches of my subjects as I crush their fingers. Listening to them plead for mercy as I pop out their eyes. Watching the tears roll down their cheeks from the empty sockets as I slit their noses. That is what takes me to the edge. Then, finally seeing the look on their faces as they realize there is no reprieve but death, well, that is what brings me to orgasm. But enough idle chatter. I want to hear a mighty scream as I first remove your right ear."

He grabbed hold of David's hair and placed the knife against his ear and began to cut. David whimpered in pain as the eunuch made the first cut, severing his lobe.

"I said scream, damn you!" yelled Lahlou, taking another hack at David's ear. David gave a shriek and twisted his neck so that his head pushed against his shoulder. It wasn't something that Lahlou had anticipated. "Lift your head, you wretch," he snarled. Then, leaning forward, he gave David's hair, which he still held in his left hand, a terrible wrench. David's head snapped back, and his right leg shot out. Guided by providence and propelled by the thought of the horrors that awaited him, his foot barreled through the layers of fat that hung from the eunuch's belly and connected with the de-scrotumed pudenda. Lahlou gave a low whistle and then toppled forward onto David, crushing him and the chair beneath his terrible weight.

For a moment, David couldn't move, but as the eunuch writhed around in pain, he was able to extract his upper body from under Lahlou. His hands were still tied to pieces of the chair, but the rope was loose, and he was able to reach Lahlou's knife, which lay next to his bald head. David quickly cut the rope and then, with a tremendous effort, pulled his legs free. As he stood up, the eunuch rolled over, and David saw that the floor was wet with Lahlou's urine and blood.

"What have you done? What have you done?" Lahlou moaned, tears rolling down his cheeks.

It was obvious to David precisely what he'd done. From the blood and torn flesh, he realized that when he'd kicked Lahlou, his foot must have driven the ruby plug into the eunuch's bladder.

"My apologies," David said, feeling a genuine pang of sorrow for the large mass of flesh that quivered with pain. "It was not my intention to make you suffer so. Though, of course, you would have done it to me."

"I can't help it," cried Lahlou as he rolled from side to side, trying to relieve the pain. "Get out of here and leave me to die. I have no wish for your company."

"Nor I yours," David said, "but I cannot leave you to die in agony." He reached down and removed the *sica* from its sheath and then, rolling the eunuch onto his side, he plunged it into the right kidney and drew it across to sever the renal artery. "There," said David, almost kindly, "your pain and suffering will soon be over."

Lahlou was dead before David had cleaned the *sica* on the eunuch's robe. A money pouch that must have been hidden in Lahlou's sleeve had fallen onto the floor. It held more than enough gold and silver coins for David to get back to Baghdad. He wrapped his scarf round his head to staunch the blood and climbed the stairs from the basement prison. The only other person in Wilkinson's house was an old crone, who was sweeping the kitchen floor. She barely looked up when she saw David.

"Your employer, Wilkinson, left a big blob of fat in the basement," he said to her. "If you stick your hand in and feel around, you'll probably find a very expensive ruby." She gave him a toothless grin as he left the house.

The warm sun reflecting off the whitewashed walls of the villas improved David's mood somewhat, but he had no idea what time it was or how he'd get off the island without Eskender or Sha, who, he assumed, had already left. He thought about what Lahlou had said about the Templar treasure. If it was true—and everything he said made it sound so, with the ruby plug only adding to the veracity of the discovery—then at the very least, he should tell the rabbi. If nothing else, it would compensate the community for the actions of the consuls and the previous governor.

He approached a man dressed in European garb strolling down the street to ask what time it was. The man shooed him off with his cane and called him a filthy beggar. At first, David had no idea why the man would address him so rudely. Then he realized how disheveled he must look with blood on his face and shoulders from his partially severed ear. The wound still throbbed, but the pain had subsided. He worried about infection when he felt a fly buzzing around his head. When he stopped to look around, he saw that he was closer to the harbor than he was to the house. As he had no clue whether Sha and Eskender had left anything there in case he returned, he walked towards the harbor.

He scanned the passengers boarding the ships but couldn't see anyone resembling a tall Ethiopian man or a blonde Circassian woman amongst the ragtag crowd of crewmen, porters, and passengers. For the first time since he'd left Baghdad, he felt truly lost and despondent. Other than the eunuch's purse, he'd lost the money he'd been owed for a job he'd failed to complete. There was a slight chance that Eskender would be able to send some of it to Ruth, but David wasn't optimistic. As close as he had become with Eskender and Sha, they were still the property of Reşid Pasha, and they'd feel obliged to return the money to him.

He contemplated the hopelessness of his situation for a few minutes, and his mind turned to Amrani Lahlou.

How had he missed the eunuch's perfidy in Constantinople? Could it be because he'd seen Lahlou as a hideous, deformed monster the first time he met him in the carriage and allowed his own bigotry to cloud his mind? He wondered how long it would take for someone to find Lahlou's body and if the old crone would be able to identify him. She didn't look capable of recognizing herself in a mirror, and Wilkinson, the only other person who knew of his presence in the house, was on his way to Acre.

For the second time in two days, he sat on a low wall and looked out at the sea beyond Mandraki Harbor. From this moment on, he decided, life was going to be difficult. Once Eskender and Sha reported his failure to Reşid Pasha, David's reputation would be immeasurably damaged, and further prospects of commissions from any official of the Ottoman Empire would be nonexistent. He could run the carpet store as a legitimate business, he supposed, unless the Ottomans decided to have him thrown in jail or executed for his failure. He continued on this path of dreary musings, feeling more and more despondent, until he was interrupted by one of the most joyous sounds he'd ever heard.

"Effendi, effendi, you are alive!"

He looked up to see Sha and Eskender walking towards him and began to cry.

Chapter 30

"What poor friends and servants we would have been to abandon you, effendi," Sha said, brushing his cheeks with a silk cloth.

"I believe I was clear in my instructions," David said, putting his hands on their shoulders.

"Your instructions were very clear," Eskender said, "and as servants, we would have obeyed them without question. But from the moment you dismissed me outside Massi's house, we were no longer your servants. As friends, we would never have abandoned you. I followed you to Wilkinson's villa, so at the very least, I knew where you were. Then I walked back to the house to help Sha get ready for our voyage. We arranged for the luggage to be taken to the docks and stored in the office of the ship's agent, and while we were waiting to see if you'd join us, we saw Wilkinson getting out of a carriage and walking toward a British steamboat."

"So, he has left already?"

"I did not see him board, but the ship departed shortly after, so I assume he was on it. From one of the stevedores, I learned it is bound for Acre."

"That part I know, and we must talk about that. The question is, how did you find me?"

"It was obvious to both of us," Sha said, "that if Wilkinson still lived, then something bad had happened to you. We hastened to Wilkinson's house and found it abandoned but for an old woman clutching a magnificent ruby, which she claimed the man in the cellar had given her. When we saw it was Amrani Lahlou, dead in a pool of blood and urine, and not you, we came back here to the harbor."

David laughed. "So, she wasn't just a hopeless old woman. Good for her." He explained the gruesome details of the ruby and how the old woman had gotten hold of it. "There is another part to what happened in the cellar relating to the ruby that I must tell you, but before I do . . . ." He opened his arms to embrace them both. "How fortunate am I to have such loyal friends. You have done more for me than anyone, but now I must impose on your generosity once again."

"You have only to ask," Sha said. Eskender nodded his agreement.

"The assignment set to me by Reşid Pasha and the young sultan is not complete while Wilkinson lives. I must go to Acre and look for an opportunity to finish him. I know nothing of the city nor what is happening there other than a few loose details from the governor."

"I can answer that easily, effendi," Eskender said. "A few weeks ago, a British, Austrian, and Ottoman fleet bombarded Acre, defeating the rebel Muhammad Ali Pasha, the Khedive of Egypt. I believe he has now agreed to various terms of surrender. Wilkinson is there to help draft the details of the terms. I do not know the current status of the city, but from what I learned a few days ago, it is a dangerous place."

"All the better, then," David said. "My ask is, then, that you accompany me to Acre for hopefully what will be a very short time. But before we go there, I must tell you what I learned from the eunuch before he began to torture me." David told them of the Templar treasure and his desire to give it to the Jews of Rhodes as reparation for the injustice of the consuls and the Greek Orthodox church.

"And you believed him?" asked Sha, who clearly didn't.

"I do. There was no reason for him to tell me a lie when he intended to kill me. Even Wilkinson sounded sincere, a characteristic I had not observed when I met him. Then there is the ruby plug."

"The lost Templar treasure is the stuff of legends," Eskender said. "Thousands have looked for it, but most scholars believed that a portion of it may have been given to the Hospitallers here on Rhodes, and the rest was lost or didn't exist. As for the ruby, well, Amrani Lahlou is, or was, someone of immense wealth. That ruby was most likely one of his personal jewels."

"You may both be right, but at the very least, I would like to go to see for myself. My only worry is if someone other than the old woman finds Lahlou's body."

"Not a concern, effendi. The door to the cellar was concealed behind a screen. We locked it and replaced the screen before we left. When the stench from his rotting corpse reaches the upper floor, we should be safely on the ship to Acre."

"That's why I need you both. You think of everything."

There was a supply ship sailing for Acre on the evening tide, and Sha bought them passage and gave the ship's captain enough money to make sure they'd be comfortable on the four-day voyage. They returned to the house, which had not yet been officially handed back to the governor. David bathed, had his ear cleaned and bandaged by Sha, and then, dressed in his official uniform, he walked with Eskender and Sha to the Jewish quarter.

Istamboli's house was not hard to find. It sat on the edge of the Jewish quarter and stood apart from the others because it was made of raw limestone that had not been covered in clay and painted like most of the other houses in the area. It was larger than the neighboring houses but had the distinct appearance of a rundown warehouse rather than a dwelling. There was a chain across the door, and a uniformed guard stood outside.

"Stand aside," Eskender said to the guard. "The *Reis ül-küttab* of the Sublime Porte demands entry."

The guard, a local thug recruited by Wilkinson from the harbor taverns, had never heard of a *Reis ül-küttab* and wasn't in the least intimidated by David's uniform. He shook his head and put his hand on the hilt of his sword.

"No one gets in but that foreign consul Wilkinson or his son or some other fat bastard who has a hard time squeezing through the door."

"How dare you speak to an emissary of the exalted Sultan Abdülmecid in that manner?"

"I'll speak to whomever I like, however I like," the guard replied, pulling the wicked-looking sword from its scabbard. "Now get—"

His words dissolved into an awful gurgle of pain as David drove his right fist into the guard's sciatic nerve and his left into his throat. He fell to the ground, where he lay paralyzed, staring in confusion at the slight man in the splendid uniform. Eskender bent down and retrieved a large key from a pouch on the guard's belt, with which he unlocked the chain and opened the door. A number of people had witnessed the event, but all except one moved on quickly, no doubt intimidated by the official whose actions were a blur but resulted in a large, armed man lying prone in the dirt. It was too soon after they'd been starved by the Ottoman officials for them to show anything but deference to anyone in uniform.

The one man who hadn't moved on watched them drag the guard into the house and shut the door. He waited for a minute and bolted off to inform the man paying him to keep vigil.

Chapter 31

It was Sha who discovered the fake wall.

At first, all they could see were the remnants of a life not well lived. Two wooden chairs stood next to a rickety table set with broken earthenware bowls and chipped plates. The dirt floor was covered in rodent feces. The back room was even more of a disaster, with a simple wooden bed and nightstand, foul-looking linen, and a wardrobe standing against the back wall. A prayer shawl and skullcap had been thrown on the floor together with two shattered clay tablets covered in Hebrew script. The wardrobe had two compartments: one for hanging items and the other with shelves, all of which were empty. There were two oil lamps on the nightstand, which Sha lit so they could examine the walls, but they could see no evidence of excavation or a false front.

"Perhaps we should ask the guard," Eskender said to David. "If he is still able to communicate."

"I doubt he will be for a while, but this makes no sense. A guard, a heavy chain, Wilkinson's son, a fat man who can barely squeeze through the door. We need to look more carefully. No doubt they have concealed their digging sufficiently so as not to arouse suspicion."

"Either that or this whole thing is a hoax," Eskender said. "But we have some time before we must return to the harbor." He and David walked back to the front room and began to examine every inch of the wall. It didn't take long for them to conclude that the walls were exactly as they'd been for hundreds of years. As David sat down on one of the wooden chairs, rubbing his forehead in frustration, Sha called to them from the back room. She stood in front of the wardrobe, from which she'd removed the back panel. Behind it was a large, dark hole.

"How could we have missed something so obvious?" David said.

"Most things are obvious once you see them," Sha replied, holding the lamp so that they could see into the hole. "It seems as if this is a passage large enough to walk through. It runs along the wall, but I see no treasure."

David took the lantern and stepped through the hole. "Wait here. I'll see if it's safe." As he stepped into what turned out to be a narrow passageway, he saw a small recess to the left and just darkness to the right. He moved cautiously, holding the lantern in front of him, doing his best not to touch the slime and mold that clung to the stone. He could tell that it had been purposefully constructed, unlike the rest of the building, which was more haphazard. The walls of the passage were thick, and the floor, unlike the trampled clay floors in the bedroom and entrance, had been paved over.

He'd taken no more than a few steps when he came to a trapdoor in the floor. The wood was old and the iron handle rusted, but it was obvious from the scuff marks that it had been recently lifted. David sensed movement behind him and saw that Eskender and Sha, holding the second lantern, had not heeded his admonition to wait. He took hold of the handle and, with Eskender's help, managed to lift the thick wooden door. In the dim light from the lantern, they could see a narrow stone staircase that disappeared into the darkness below.

"Now I really do need you to listen to me," David said. "Let me go down first. If there is danger below, then we'll need someone up here to help. Sha, you stay here at the trapdoor, and Eskender, you retreat to the end of the passage and conceal yourself in the recess in case Wilkinson's son or one of his henchmen decides to come and investigate."

This time, they both listened. David stepped cautiously onto the steps and climbed down, holding the lantern in front of him. The staircase descended no more than six feet into a small chamber that was stacked with rotting wooden chests. Half of them were open and empty of whatever had been inside. The wood on those chests that remained closed was rotted through, and the lids came off easily. Inside the first were hundreds of coins. He could tell they were ancient. Some looked like dinars with Arabic verse. Others bore Christian symbols, but all were gold. Of that, he was sure. He opened another chest, which contained jewel-encrusted crucifixes and chalices. There were more gold coins in the third, and the fourth one he opened was filled with jewels.

David had seen large collections of valuables before, but nothing, not even those in the sultan's palace in

Constantinople, rivaled the treasure that lay before him. His mind began to swim at the possibilities that such wealth could bring. Just one of the chests of gold coins would be enough for him to move his family from Baghdad to Bombay like his old friend David Sassoon, the great merchant prince. His chest began to heave, and his palms felt clammy. He waited a moment until visions of a life filled with the trappings of prosperity vanished and then called out to Sha to join him. She said nothing when she saw what the chests contained, but the light from the lantern caught the excitement in her eyes. She picked up a clear green stone the size of a pigeon egg.

"An emerald," she said quietly, "of immeasurable value." As she placed the stone back into the chest, there was a scream, and the body of a man tumbled down the stairs onto the stone floor of the treasure room, where it lay groaning awfully. A handgun lay at his side, and a long bayonet-style knife was buried in his left calf. Then Eskender came down the stairs. He whistled when he saw the chests.

"Who in the name of God is this?" David asked, kneeling next to the prone figure staring up at him in pain and fear.

"I am not certain," Eskender replied, kneeling next to David, "but judging by his age and European-style clothing, I suspect it might be the son of Wilkinson. His knife must have entered his leg when he fell."

The young man—David reckoned he couldn't be more than nineteen or twenty—blinked when Eskender said the name "Wilkinson."

"Help me, please," he said in English. "I don't want to die."

"We will help you," David replied, checking to see whether the knife had severed an artery, "but as to your dying, that is up to your creator." He pulled the bayonet from the young man's calf and was relieved to see that blood did not gush out. The man gave a low moan and fainted. David took the knife and cut strips from his linen shirt, and Sha, who was more skilled than he in tending to wounds, took the strips and bound the leg.

"His wrist may be broken too," she said, "judging by the angle of his hand."

"Are you going to kill him?" asked Eskender, looking at the treasure. "If this is what's left, imagine what he and his father have already taken."

"No, I won't kill him," David said, "despite his father's and his role in tormenting the Jews. But I confess I am at odds with what we should do with him."

"Just slit his throat," Sha said. "He may be young, but he is already corrupted. The world has too many of his kind."

The young man had woken just as Sha made her pronouncement. "I beg you, no," he murmured through his pain. "Please just get me home. My name is Arthur Wilkinson, and my father, who is a powerful man, will reward you."

"We know who your father is," David said, "and the only reward he would offer us is torture and death, as he tried to do to me just hours before he left for Acre. No, the only way out for you, my boy, is to tell us where the rest of the treasure is."

"I don't know what you're talking about . . . what treasure?"

"Let me adjust your hand for you," said Eskender, bending the fingers of the broken hand.

Arthur screamed, tears rolling down his cheeks. "Look," said David gently. "No one wants to hurt you. But we are not fools. You came here deliberately to see what we were doing. Both your father and the eunuch told me, as they began to torture me, that you had already removed half of the treasure. So, if you want us to help you, and you have my assurance that we will, just tell me where you put the rest of the treasure. If you don't, I promise you, we will remove what is here and leave you to rot in this dark room. Your death will be neither quick nor pleasant. We may leave you enough water to survive for a few days so that you can experience the pain of your leg rotting. Or you can tell us where the treasure is, and we will deliver you into the care of someone who will clean your wound and set your hand. The choice is yours."

"The treasure is in a secret room in my father's house, where Amrani Lalou was staying. It is behind a screen in his study. If you help me out of here, I will show you. Now, please, I am in great pain."

"We will help you out, but unfortunately not to your father's house."

David and Eskender carried the young man up the stairs and through the passage into the bedroom, where they laid him on the bed. Sha waited with him while David and Eskender went to see the rabbi.

"Are you sure you want to do this?" asked Eskender after David explained what he planned to do with the treasure. "You could be wealthy beyond your dreams."

"No. I thought about it briefly, but I came to do a job for which I will be amply compensated once I have taken care of Wilkinson. There is a curse on my family that goes back close to two millennia. It doesn't mention unearned compensation that I know of—only that we must live by the *sica* until the seventieth generation—but why would I take a chance? However, I must insist that you and Sha take a portion so that you can buy your freedom, as I understand Ottoman slaves can do."

"Your generosity, effendi, is only exceeded by your skills with that dagger. But you should understand that both Sha and I could buy our freedom whenever we like, together or alone, as we are both fairly compensated by Reşid Pasha. Perhaps we will one day, but he, like you, is a generous and indulgent master who treats us like his own family and allows us freedoms that we would not otherwise experience, slaves or not. Perhaps, however, we will each choose one thing that will remind us of this time."

It was the first time Eskender had spoken about his relationship with Sha, and David wanted to know more. But before he could ask, Eskender stopped him. "Here we are at the synagogue."

Chapter 32

R abbi Israel was still prone when David and Eskender entered his chamber.

"*Reis ül-küttab,*" he said, "once again forgive my manners. I am still not able to stand, though the doctor says I am mending. Please take a seat."

"I am glad that the doctor is optimistic, Rabbi, and hopefully what I am about to tell you will add greatly to that optimism. This, by the way, is Eskender, a secretary to the great Reşid Pasha. His assistance to me here in Rhodes cannot be measured in mere words."

"Welcome, Eskender," the rabbi said, giving him a polite smile. "May I offer you both refreshment?"

After a servant had brought in coffee and pastries, David moved his chair closer to the divan on which the rabbi reclined. "Last time we met, I told you I'd look into the issue of the mysterious men who visited the house of poor Istamboli."

"Ah, yes," said the rabbi, looking quite serious. "I am eager to hear what you found out. It was reported to me no more than a few hours ago that a man bearing your description overpowered a guard at the house with a move that was 'faster than the eye could follow.' At least that's how it was related to me." He gave David a wry grin. "I must tell you I laughed when I heard it, as I find it almost incomprehensible that a man as dignified as the *Reis ül-küttab* could be capable of such behavior."

"In my position," David replied with a grin that matched the rabbi's in wryness, "I have learned not to give too much credence to the testimony of eyewitnesses. However, it's true that Eskender and I, together with our colleague, Sha, did enter the house of Istamboli, where we discovered precisely what it was that the mysterious visitors had discovered."

"And?"

"It is a treasure trove that must have once belonged to the Knights Hospitaller before their sudden expulsion to Malta." David held up his hand to stop the rabbi, who was about to say something. "Please, before you ask any questions, let me first elaborate on what I told you last time. I said that I was sent here by Reşid Pasha and the sultan to ensure that the Jewish community of Rhodes would not need rescuing again."

"Those were the very words you used, and you asked me to think of you as a golem."

"I did, and it appears that all of the consuls, bar one, have somehow fallen victim to The Golem."

"Again, *Reis ül-küttab,* that is what I have heard. You know, I never believed in the golem, but it appears I was wrong. In the stories, it is usually the rabbi who conjures up the golem. As it wasn't me, it must be some other rabbi who has come into the community while I have been laid up. But you mentioned a treasure?" The skepticism in the

Rabbi's voice made David uncomfortable. He looked over at Eskender, but the Ethiopian's face was impassive.

"Yes, it is a vast amount of money that I am going to turn over to you and your congregation in compensation for what you have endured. It will take a number of strong men to remove it from the secret underground room in Istamboli's house, and I advise you to move fast before thieves appear." He explained to the Rabbi precisely where the treasure was hidden, and after some discussion, the rabbi, still dubious, agreed to send two men he trusted to see it for themselves.

"There is just one more thing," he said to the rabbi before he, Eskender, and the two men left for the house. "A young man who behaved badly towards your congregation in the past lies severely injured in Istamboli's house. He needs the attention of a doctor, which I hope you will provide."

"Of course. If he is young and injured, we will tend to him no matter what his past is. He will experience no animosity from us."

"You may experience it from him, but I am certain you can handle that. I will see your men to the house, and then we must leave Rhodes. I wish you a fast recovery and peace in the years to come. I hope the treasure serves you well."

"Thank you, *Reis ül-küttab*. I don't know who you are, and I can't say I approve of everything you have done—"

"If indeed I did anything. When we first met, you wondered if God had chosen the Jews for any other purpose than to suffer. Maybe the treasure is His way of compensating you."

David and Eskender walked with the rabbi's two men to Istamboli's house. They were met by Sha, who seemed less than enthusiastic about Arthur Wilkinson's chances of recovery without immediate medical attention.

"He'll get more than he deserves," Eskender said. "But we must hurry if we still want to find the rest of the treasure. Our ship leaves in a matter of hours." They told the two men where to look and heard muted but excited cries when they found it. Then they left the Jewish quarter for Wilkinson's house.

"And what are we to do with the treasure at Wilkinson's house, if his son was not lying to us?" Eskender asked.

"After you each choose your jewels, we'll stop at the governor's house and tell him that he is to send the treasure to the Sublime Porte and to arrest Wilkinson, or whatever the laws of diplomacy allow, should he ever show up in Rhodes again. We won't mention what we gave to the rabbi."

The rest of the treasure was where Arthur had said it would be. There were six chests bound with rope that Wilkinson and his son had used to stop the rotting wood from falling apart. Three of the chests contained gold coins, two were filled with sacred artifacts, and the sixth with jewels even more magnificent than those in Istamboli's house.

The house itself was empty, and the secret door to the dungeon where the eunuch's body lay was still locked and concealed behind the screen. David waited in the courtyard while Sha and Eskender chose their reward. For no more than a few seconds, the thought of great wealth once again filled his head and then vanished like mist before the sun, and he knew that all he wanted at that moment was to get back to Baghdad to see Ruth and the children, though the thought of how he'd face Ruth and what he'd say filled him with terror.

He didn't have long to wait for Sha and Eskender, neither of whom showed him what they'd chosen. Seeing as neither carried a large container, it couldn't have been much.

"How will you explain the discovery to the governor?" Eskender asked.

"I won't. I'll just tell him that it exists and that he should take some for local taxes to cover the cost of the events of the past few months and to send the rest to Constantinople. I have no doubt he'll keep most for himself, and what remains will go to the Sublime Porte, who I'm sure you'll agree won't miss what isn't there from a treasure no one even knew existed."

Chapter 33

The ship that Eskender had managed to secure was an old Venetian trabàccolo. Like a host of small cargo ships sailing the Adriatic, it was taking supplies to the now-occupied Syrian city of Acre, where a combined British and Austrian force had defeated Muhammad Ali, the ruler of Egypt on behalf of the Ottomans. The trabàccolo was not—despite the captain's assurances—a passenger ship, and where the extra money that Sha had provided went to ensure their comfort was not immediately obvious.

"Acre looks like a city on which the old gods danced a tarantella," the captain said to his passengers, who were seated on bales of cloth covered in sheepskins under a canopy made from an old sail. "Not a city I'd choose to visit were it not a place to make more money than I've made in years. The British and Austrians don't know the price of anything, and what remains of the Egyptian army will pay whatever they have for a crust of bread."

"So, what you're saying is that you're a cheat and a thief," Sha said, shaking her head.

"What does a woman know of trading?" laughed the captain. "I'm neither a cheat nor a thief. Simply a businessman who takes advantage of an opportunity. Tell me one rich man who hasn't done the same. If we were governed by our conscience, we'd all be poor. And thank you for your thoughts, but I have no wish to ever be poor again."

"This is the second time in a matter of weeks that I've had to ask this," David said. "Doesn't your religion claim that it is easier for a camel to pass through the eye of a needle than it is for a rich man to enter what you call heaven?"

"Spare me the banality," the captain replied. "The trouble with self-righteous people is that they always have a pithy quotation from The Bible or some old Greek philosopher to express their disapproval of someone who has something they don't have but want. No, my friends, just because something sounds erudite doesn't mean it is. If we are all created in the image of God, then am I not doing precisely what He would do? There, was that a more satisfactory answer to your question than the last one provided?" He didn't wait for a response. "Now, I hope you enjoy the quarters I've rigged up for you for the duration of the trip. We have a fair wind, and I expect to see Acre within three days at most."

"What a disagreeable man," Sha said when the captain had left to attend to a loose sail.

"Perhaps," David said, "but he is a practical man, and in my experience it's his kind that make things happen rather than the dreamers and idealists, who'd starve if it weren't for our captain and those who share his philosophy."

Starving was not an issue on the voyage. The ship's cook made huge bowls of what he called "spaghetti" with tomato sauce and fish. Though difficult to eat, it was delicious and filling. The winter sun warmed them during the day, but nights were cold, and the canopy provided little shelter from the frequent squalls that skipped across the Levantine Sea. Extra sheepskins provided by the captain made the nights bearable, and on the third day, a crewman in the crow's nest yelled out something that sounded like "Acre."

David counted twenty-one warships anchored in front of the city, which fitted perfectly the captain's description of a place destroyed in a tarantella performed by ancient gods. Most of the warships were British, but a few displayed the Ottoman standard, and two had a flag recognized by Eskender as belonging to the Empire of Austria.

"That large gun ship, *The Princess Charlotte*, is commanded by the British Admiral Sir Robert Stopford, and that one by the Archduke Friedrich of Austria, who led the landing party. A nasty piece of work by all accounts but brave, I suppose, for one born to privilege." The captain shook his head and turned to yell at one of the crew.

They marveled at the huge ships for a moment and then watched the myriad smaller cargo boats, some anchored alongside the warships and others sailing nimbly through the fleet towards the harbor. Everywhere they looked, they saw only destruction. The buildings surrounding the harbor had been reduced to rubble, the breakwater wall was severely damaged, and what remained of a fortification that the captain described as the great Tower of Flies lay utterly demolished.

"I will try to get us as close as possible to the harbor," the captain said, "and then you will have to go ashore in one of the rowboats. You can see them going back and forth with goods and passengers. Of course, they will try to rob you blind if you display any weakness, but I've always found a swift kick to the groin provides wondrous results."

David wished the captain good trading, and Sha gave him a nasty sneer. Eskender, who was ambivalent to the whims of merchants, hailed a rowboat, and twenty minutes later, the trio scrambled ashore in what was one of the oldest continuously occupied cities in the world. Once the stronghold of the Crusaders and ruled at various times by Egyptians, Phoenicians, and Ottomans, it was now just a sad testament to the ravaging of shells and explosives. Sha secured them rooms at a small inn that had somehow escaped the British bombardment and the attention of drunken sailors. While she and David settled in, Eskender went out to get a lay of the land. He was back an hour later with news.

"I have two pieces of news, effendi, that will affect your plans if indeed you have any at this early stage. First, Wilkinson is here and staying in a large house occupied by the British delegation. From one of the servants, I learned that he is keen to return to Rhodes as soon as possible."

"Then I shall hasten his return—though not to Rhodes."

"I thought you'd say that. The other piece of news is that Reşid Pasha will be arriving the day after tomorrow to represent the Sublime Porte at the treaty discussions. It will be a good thing for all of us if Wilkinson is gone by then."

David was not given to low whistles, but this seemed like the perfect occasion for one. "Then I'd best move as quickly as possible. Can you show me the house where Wilkinson is staying?"

"Yes, but you should also know that there are patrols of soldiers on the lookout for any of Muhammad Ali's troops who still roam the streets looking for mischief. If they see you dressed like you are in the robes of a *bashi-bazouk*, they will certainly take you to the jail for questioning. And from what I understand, few who enter emerge in one piece."

"As always, Eskender, your advice and caution are more valuable even than the treasure we discovered. Well, then, Sha, hopefully you brought my *Reis ül-küttab* uniforms?"

Before Sha could answer, Eskender held up his hand. "I would not suggest that, effendi. There are a few Ottoman officials aboard the ships, and if they saw you in the uniform of a senior representative of the Porte, they would ask too many questions. My suggestion is that you wear your stambouline. That way, you can pass yourself off as a Baghdadi merchant come to explore the market for goods to trade in Acre. The patrols will not harass someone dressed in Western garb."

Eskender's council would have proved to be correct if he hadn't overestimated the intelligence of a typical British Marine corporal.

Eskender and David—dressed in his black frock coat, grey trousers, and a dark blue fez—hadn't gone more than a few blocks from the inn when they were stopped by a four-man patrol of marines in their red jackets and bell-top shakos.

"And where are you two buggers off to?" said the corporal, slamming his Brunswick rifle across David's chest.

David held up his hands as if to stop the corporal. "There is no need for violence, sir. I am a merchant from Baghdad, come to ensure a fair trade in goods to help repair this broken city." David did his best to look indignant, but the corporal, who'd seen "indignant" many times before on the face of his sergeant, dismissed him with an even harder shove.

"Oh yeah, come to see what you can steal more likely ... and who's this?" He pointed his bayonet at Eskender. "Ali Baba?"

"He is my clerk," David replied, trying to sound confident though not feeling it. "And you have no right to accuse us of being thieves. I am an important businessman."

"Let's see how important you feel after my sergeant puts you through his paces at the jail. Alright, me lads, let's march these two croakers off to the nick."

"I must protest," David said as he was given a shove by one of the marines. "This is most unnecessary."

"I'll show you unnecessary," said the soldier, smashing the stock of his Brunswick into David's back. As he stumbled forward, a man stepped out of a house not four feet away and immediately stopped in his tracks. David looked at him and his heart sank. It was Wilkinson.

For a moment, Wilkinson just stared at him, and then he stepped up to the corporal. "Where are you taking these two vagabonds?"

The corporal, who knew a man of authority when he saw one, touched his knuckles to his forehead in the traditional salute and held up his arm to stop the procession. "We're taking them in for interrogation, sah. And they ain't gonna enjoy it."

"I've a better idea, Corporal: shoot them right here against that wall. I give you permission."

"I don't know about that, sah ... might be a bit extreme. Don't you worry, though. We'll give 'em a good booting back at the jail."

Before Wilkinson, who looked extremely anxious, could respond, David took a step forward. "Both of those suggestions will be to the disadvantage of your son, Wilkinson."

The soldier nearest David raised his rifle and swung the stock at David's head. Much to his surprise, though the surprise lasted no more than a second, it missed entirely as he fell to the ground, paralyzed from a blow to the sciatic nerve followed by one to his neck that left him unconscious. The action was so quick that the corporal and the other two soldiers, who had no idea what they'd just seen, froze. It was Wilkinson who broke the proverbial ice.

"My son! What about my son?" He put a restraining hand on the corporal, who'd recovered sufficiently from the shock of seeing one of his men toppled like a stuck pig and was about to skewer David with his bayonet.

"Perhaps, Mr. Wilkinson," David said, "you'd prefer to discuss the matter in private. I assure you it will be worth your while."

Wilkinson hesitated, not quite sure what to say.

"If your son's situation does not concern you sufficiently, I also have a letter written to Sir Robert Stopford detailing, should we say, your 'proclivity,' that will be delivered by one of my associates should we not return safely."

That did the trick as far as Wilkinson was concerned. "Corporal," he said, "I fear you have made a mistake with these two men. They are well-known to me, and I will vouch for them should your sergeant ask."

"Very well, sah, but what about Featherington here?" He nudged the downed marine with his boot. "I can't allow that to go unpunished."

"If a big burly fellow like Featherington can't take care of himself, then you have a very poor squad, Corporal. Now pick him up, and away with you. I have business with these two, uh, gentlemen."

The corporal made a grumbling sound, signaled the three other marines to pick up the unfortunate Featherington, and left Wilkinson alone with David and Eskender.

"You filthy blackmailing swine," Wilkinson said, clenching his fist and stamping his foot like an upset child.

David shook his head and smiled. "Fine words coming from a murdering thief. But before you throw a tantrum and attract more soldiers, why don't we find somewhere private so I can tell you what I need from you?"

"Very well," Wilkinson said, "but my son had better be safe, and you had better not try anything, or you'll know my wrath."

"I already know your wrath, Wilkinson, and I have no fear of it. Your son is safe for the moment, which is more than I can say for your friend Amrani Lahlou, whose body lies rotting in your cellar. And as for trying anything, you need have no fear. I won't be expending any effort in what I have to do or say. Now come along." They turned off the main thoroughfare into what must have been a residential street before the bombardment but was now a row of ruined and seemingly abandoned houses.

Eskender, who hadn't said a word until now, hesitated when David steered them into a house that was no more than three walls and rubble where the fourth had been.

"Effendi, perhaps I should stand outside to keep watch. I—"

"Good idea, Eskender. What I have to say to Mr. Wilkinson is for his ears only. Then we can both see him back to his lodgings."

Eskender nodded, knowing full well what was about to happen and relieved that he wouldn't have to witness it.

"Look," said Wilkinson when he and David were alone. "I'm sorry about what happened with the eunuch. I'm glad you escaped, and in truth, I'm happy he's dead. He was a fat, greedy bastard who would have cheated me out of everything. I will reward you handsomely if you don't harm me or my son. Now tell me what you think would be a fair sum for my son's safety, and, um, the destruction of that letter you spoke of."

David waited patiently as the consul pleaded with him. He felt no remorse at what he was about to do. Whether Wilkinson's actions merited retribution was not his decision to make. Judgment had already been passed by the emperor of the Ottoman Empire.

"Let me put your mind at ease," he said softly. "Your son is perfectly safe as far as I know and is being cared for by some of the Jews you did your best to torture and kill."

"But . . . but . . . they'll murder him."

"I don't believe so. Not everyone is filled with hatred as great as yours."

"No, they'll sacrifice him! That's what they do to Christian children."

"You don't really believe that. I know you and the other consuls took the boy you claimed had been slaughtered by the Jews to another island and paid his parents handsomely to lie to the authorities."

Wilkinson looked as if he was about to deny it, and then he shook his head. "It doesn't matter now. I just want to go home and see my son. Please, I beg you. I will make you richer than—"

"Than who? Than you would be when you sell the treasure?" David watched as Wilkinson's face fell. "Unfortunately, it is no longer yours. I gave the Jews of Rhodes almost all the treasure from the secret room in Istamboli's house, and the rest—the horde you already removed to your own abode—I handed over to the governor to send to Constantinople."

Wilkinson gaped like a dying fish. Then his face moved through the emotional color spectrum from the white of fear to the red of anger and finally the purple of rage.

"No," he shrieked. "You can't do that. It's mine! I found it!"

His next words were more of a gurgle than a scream as the *sica* sliced through both kidneys in a fluid motion. Wilkinson put his hand on David's arm to steady himself and then crumpled to the floor, where he lay in a pool of blood, staring at the man he'd believed was already dead.

David's only regret was that he didn't have a clay golem to leave by the consul's body. He wiped the *sica* on Wilkinson's shirt, replaced it in its sheath, and walked out to where Eskender stood watch.

"It's done then?" asked the Ethiopian, looking relieved

"It is. I'm pleased to say my assignment is complete. It's time for me to go home."

THE GOLEM

Chapter 34

W hen David and Eskender got back to the inn, they found Sha setting out food and wine on the wooden table in their quarters.

They ate mostly in silence, contemplating all they'd shared and preparing themselves for the inevitable parting. When they were finished with the simple meal, David took each of their hands.

"This was our final meal together," he said. "Tomorrow, the pasha will arrive, and he will no doubt be keen to reconnect with you. I hope your report satisfies him, and his trust and confidence in you grow, as they should. You were the best of companions. Do not make my role too impressive, as I have no desire to take on another of his assignments—unless, of course, it would mean working with both of you again."

"In that case, effendi, we will make you sound like the greatest warrior of all time," Eskender said.

"Yes," Sha added, her smile as seductive and alluring as it had been in the hammam. "Your actions and technique would be legendary in my own country should I ever get there to tell it."

David gave an embarrassed laugh. "Ah, well, who knows what providence has in mind for us in the future? I will try to slip out of the city tonight before Wilkinson's body is discovered and those Marines come looking for me. I believe you'll be safe, Eskender, for your face was partially wrapped, and their focus was on me rather than you."

"I assumed you'd be leaving us tonight," Sha said, standing up and walking over to a rickety closet. "I bought this large saddlebag in which I have put your fee from the sultan, along with what few clothes you have. It is heavy, I must warn you."

"Thank you. As I said, you and Eskender think of everything. I will no doubt need a horse or a camel, even, and a guide, as I have no idea how to get home."

Once again, Sha provided the solution. "There is a caravan leaving the city later tonight headed for Damascus. Arrangements have been made for you to travel with them. One of the guards will come to the inn to collect you in a few hours. He has a pass that will get you through the city to the east gate, where you will join the others."

They sat together talking and laughing and drinking wine like old friends until the innkeeper knocked on the door to say that the caravan guard had come to collect David.

When they'd said their goodbyes and Eskender had gone to his room, Sha presented David with a small leather pouch.

"Inside," she said, "is a gift that a loving husband would take to his wife. No, don't open it till you are alone and in a secure place away from the eyes of thieves." David was almost in tears. He leaned forward to kiss her, but she pulled away. "You are no longer the *Reis ül-küttab.* You are once again David Smulian-Hasson, loving and faithful husband, who would not be tempted by an enchantress. Even one as beautiful as me."

"Before I leave," David said, "and please forgive me if it sounds like I am prying into your affairs, but what of you and Eskender?"

"What of us?" asked Sha, sounding not in the least put out.

"Well, it feels to me as if you would be a perfect couple."

"We are, but only as friends who would do anything for each other. We cannot be lovers as Eskender is also a eunuch . . . I see the surprise, or is it horror, on your face," She laughed. "Not all eunuchs allow the cruelty of their disfigurement to foul their minds like Lahlou. Eskender is good and kind and wise beyond words." And with that, she turned and walked out of the room before David could say another word.

The trip to Baghdad took the best part of seven weeks. The caravan of merchants was large and well-guarded, which was just as well, as the countryside was filled with armed deserters and other mischief makers. He left the caravan in Damascus and joined another to cross the Syrian Desert to Aleppo.

One night when he was sure that everyone but the guards was asleep, he opened the pouch that Sha had given him. Inside was a huge gemstone. He didn't know what it was, and he couldn't tell the color in the light of the waning moon, but he had an idea it was immensely valuable and thought that it must have come from the Templar treasure. He brought it up to his lips and closed his eyes, and for a moment, he was transported into the arms of the beautiful Circassian woman. Then his mind cleared, and he knew that Ruth was the only woman he'd ever truly love.

The caravan reached Aleppo a few weeks later. There, David paid to join a group of Yezidi clerics who were headed to Mosul on a pilgrimage. By the time he arrived in Mosul, exhausted and sore from the hard leather saddle, he swore he'd never sit on a camel again.

Fortunately, he was able to get passage on a small sailing vessel taking a consignment of silks to Baghdad. Forty-eight days after he'd said goodbye to Eskender and Sha, he jumped from the ship and made his way to his family's neighborhood in Shorjah. He carried the heavy saddlebag and small leather pouch to the carpet store, where he stood for a moment in the last light of evening, watching his son and daughter playing together. Inside, he could just see Ruth arranging a pile of small carpets, and his heart began to beat like the drum of a whirling dervish. Then the door opened, and Ruth came out to call the children for their evening meal. She glanced up for just a second, stopped, and then looked again as her husband began to run towards her.

It was a glorious homecoming as they all sat together eating lamb stewed in pomegranate molasses with rice and apricots. He told them of Constantinople and Rhodes and how he'd met the Emperor of the Ottoman Empire in his magnificent palace and people from all over the world.

"That reminds me," Ruth said as they cleared the table. "It couldn't have been more than a day or two after you'd left for Constantinople that a foreign man whose accent I'd never heard before and who styled himself a count or some such title arrived at our door. He wanted to engage your services, and when I told him you'd already left, he became quite belligerent and rude. I have no idea what happened to him after I saw him off."

"Aha," David said. "That answers a question that's troubled me ever since Rhodes. Yes, he was a very rude and belligerent man who also insulted a female passenger on the ship from Constantinople to Rhodes. A woman you would have liked, Ruth. I have a very good idea what happened to him, and I doubt he'll be rude to anyone ever again." Ruth didn't even ask why. She had no wish to know. Much later, when the children were asleep and he and Ruth had made love, he gave her the pouch with the jewel.

When she opened it, she burst into tears and hugged him. "What did I do to deserve such a wonderful gift?" she asked, kissing him on the lips as many times as she could before he pushed her away, laughing.

He wanted to say it wasn't what she'd done as much as what he'd done, but he kept quiet, and if, in the years that followed before his untimely death from cholera, she saw betrayal in his eyes or felt it in her heart, she said nothing but loved him ever after.

THE GOLEM

Epilogue

The precious stone that David gave Ruth had to have been the 12-carat Imperial Topaz that my sister now has secured in a bank vault. She got it from my mother, who wore it often. How it came into her possession is a mystery, but I suspect it was included when my mother's grandfather handed her the Smulian *sica* that had arrived in a package from Russia. I am still at odds as to how it got to Russia from Argentina, but I suspect I will find out at some point.

I did wonder, after his frequent references to his conflicted conscience, how David managed to keep silent for the few years he had left with Ruth, but I found that out, too, when I received the notes from Mozelle Hasson-Herrera in Buenos Aires that led to the writing of *The Carpet Salesman from Baghdad*, which details the adventures of Ruth and David's son Elias in India. Ruth, obviously unbeknownst to David, had had an affair with the great merchant prince David Sassoon before his expulsion from Baghdad. I always thought it was my father's family who didn't give a fig for fidelity or the sanctimony of marriage, not my mother's, pious bunch that they claim to be.

I would like to have known whether David and *Boluk-bashi* Djemal Fidan, the brave captain charged with getting David to Constantinople, ever saw each other again in Baghdad. They seemed to have developed a close friendship on the journey. I found a reference to a Chorbaji (or colonel) Djemal Fidan, who died in the Montenegrin—Ottoman War of 1852-1853. Of course, there could have been two people with the same name.

There is a rather obscure reference to Eskender that my friend, the scholar Mehmet Lüle, discovered in a paper delivered to the Syrian Scientific Society in 1869, which had recently been reestablished courtesy of the great Reşid Pasha by a Professor Muhammad Ali al-Fattah. In the paper, the professor references the brilliance of the Tanzimat Reforms and gives credit to a number of people, including Eskender. As for Sha, I could find nothing, but I have a distinct feeling that she became someone of prominence, certainly behind the scenes if not in front of them.

Even though the story is not about the Rhodean Jews who faced the Nazis and succumbed to the Holocaust like so many millions of European Jews, I know that the same spirit and strength they showed in 1944 was there when they faced the corrupt consuls of 1840. If you ever get to meet Noni, I think you'll know what I mean.

Acknowledgements

There are so many people I'd like to thank for helping me with *The Golem of Rhodes*.

First, my editor, agent, and friend, Melissa Mazzeo, who has been such a stalwart companion in my journey as a writer. Second, my old friend and colleague, the brilliant Luis Silva Dias, who has designed all my book covers. Each one is a little gem that captures both the humor and the content.

To my two sons, Simon and Steven, their wives Tracey and Lisa, and the newest addition to our family, Alexi: I love you all, and thanks for always being there with encouragement.

Finally, to all the readers who've bought my books. Every penny goes to various animal and environmental charities.

My best to you all,
Jonathan

A note from the author

Thank you so much for reading my book. I hope you enjoyed reading it as much as I enjoyed writing it. If you liked the book, I would be so appreciative if you would take a moment to leave a review for me on Amazon. Every review counts! And since all of my book sales are donated to animal charities, I know the animals will thank you as well.

Please also check out my FREE starter library, including short story Death by Green Monkey and full-length novel Infatuation, only at www.jonathanharriesink.com

DEATH BY GREEN MONKEY

BY JONATHAN HARRIES

Thirty-five years before the fateful reunion with Freddy Blank in Paris, Roger Storm was living into Johannesburg—and his larger-than-life friends are already getting him into trouble! Check out Roger Storm's first brush with a near-death experience, totally free at my website!

How far would you go for love at first sight? When Charley Brooks catches a glimpse of the voluptuous belly dancer Fanny Packer by chance in a magazine, forces beyond reason lead him to set aside his life in New York City with his perfect fiancée to chase the woman of his dreams. A mysterious book, a homicidal dwarf, a dominatrix, and a brothel on wheels all feature in this love story on acid that finds Fanny and Charley in each other's arms in this life–and maybe even into the next one.

Also by Jonathan Harries

The Roger Storm Books

KILLING HARRY BONES

BY JONATHAN HARRIES

Roger Storm, drinking heavily and contemplating suicide after his divorce and unceremonious firing from a high-powered job, gets the shock of his life when he meets his childhood friend, Freddy Blank, years after his supposed death. Roger soon finds himself dragged kicking and screaming into an adventure where a mysterious international organization is taking out poachers and trophy hunters in precisely the same ways they take out animals. Don't miss this hugely inventive, action-packed, hilarious debut novel from Jonathan Harries!

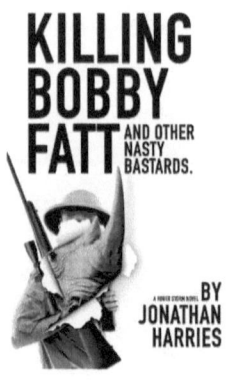

Roger Storm is back in this thrilling second book in the series! The bucolic peace of Hunter's Folly Private Game Reserve is shattered by the discovery of a noseless hunter next to a hornless rhino carcass, sending Roger on another mad adventure helping his friends to take down one of the most vicious animal trafficking rings in the world—and helping the animals to fight back!

On a remote hunting preserve in Namibia, a brilliant Indian geneticist is facing a rather nasty end unless he can find a way for elephants to grow longer tusks, rhinos bigger horns, and lions thicker manes. Behind this dastardly scheme is the notorious Russian oligarch Valerian Zolotov and members of Bratva, the Russian mafia. But there's an equally dangerous group determined to save the geneticist and put a permanent stop to these rotters.

Tales of the Sica

I had absolutely no intention of getting into the family business. As I told my father the night he enlightened me on what my ancestors had been up to for over a thousand years, "Sticking a curved dagger into someone's liver ain't quite my cup of tea." As it turned out, I had no choice. When your family's been assassinating reprobates and other loathsome individuals for seventy generations, you have a certain obligation.

Can you blame a chap for wanting to turn his otherwise humdrum family into a bunch of assassins? It turns out you can. I found this out soon after my novel The Tailor of Riga was published, and I received a bunch of beastly emails and threats from incensed family members horrified that I'd portrayed them as the descendants of bloodthirsty hitmen. Then, out of the blue, a package arrived from a long-lost cousin in Argentina that changed everything.

THE ANOTHER TALE OF THE SICA
BODYGUARD
OF
SARAWAK
BY JONATHAN HARRIES

When the British Secret Service Bureau commissioned my great-uncle Leon to whack a Russian Count aboard the SS Gwalior on its way from Cape Town to Mombasa, he had no idea the size of the maelstrom into which he was about to plunge. After tossing out bodies to the lions of Tsavo in Kenya, graduating with honors from a school specializing in sexual techniques in Singapore, avoiding headhunters in the sweltering jungles of Sarawak, to becoming bodyguard to his highness Charles Brooke, the 2nd Rajah of Sarawak, Leon carves a magnificent swath of death and seduction as the 68th generation in our family assassination business.

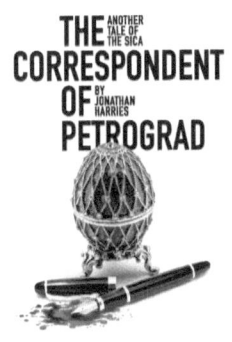

THE ANOTHER TALE OF THE SICA
CORRESPONDENT
OF BY JONATHAN HARRIES
PETROGRAD

It's the spring of 1912 and my great-uncle Leon, freshly returned to London after his assignments for the British Secret Service Bureau in Africa and Asia—including a crash course in sexual technique at the Heavenly Abode of the Crimson Lotus—is ready to settle down. Against overwhelming odds and with the assistance of the mysterious Mata Hari, Leon takes out a double agent in Vienna, dispatches a Turkish brothel-owning spy in Hamburg, and ends up in Petrograd, where his hitherto unknown involvement in the death of Rasputin is finally revealed.